THE
DANGLING
WIRE

PR HERSEY

THE DANGLING WIRE

BY PR HERSEY

She may be reached at **prhersey@juno.com**

Cover painting by Dave Thekan
Cover background photo by Laura Ashton

Cover design & book layout by Laura Ashton
laura@gitflorida.com

Author's photo, p. 239, by Paul "Fuzz" Legere

Second Edition

ISBN: 978-1479188215

Printed in the United States of America

Dedication

To my family for all their love and support, and to my life partner, Paul, for accompanying me on life's journey. I wouldn't be here without you all.

Thank you to Timmy and *The Dottie Mae*, Norma and Doctor B. In one way or another you have each made important contributions to my writing and this novel. I am grateful and thank you with all my heart.

This book is especially dedicated to my mentors and dearest friends, Pat and Victoria Miele, without whose friendship and support, I could not do the writing that I love. I will never be able to adequately thank them for all they've done for me but I will be eternally grateful. And I hope we all live long and healthy lives so that I have plenty of time to show them my gratitude!

CHAPTER ONE

I didn't think things could get worse but I knew I couldn't count on it... With some trepidation, I let my twelve year-old German Shepherd out the screen door and made my way fifty or so yards to retrieve the mail. I was getting close to discontinuing our daily trips to the mail box but these days this was the only exercise we got. I'd already stopped answering the phone.

Bounder limped lethargically beside me. His pace and general demeanor accurately reflected my own lack of enthusiasm. Apparently we were both feeling the effects of a rough year and passionless life. It seemed there was no meaning in living anymore and there had not been since the death of my parents—Bounder's real masters.

The mail box stood on a post on the opposite side of the dirt road in front of our driveway. Without thinking, I stepped on to the road. Putting one foot in front of the other I went about the business of existing. Faithfully, Bounder plodded along beside me. Halfway across the road, I realized I was considering suicide. Instead of being shocked, I was amazed; the mere thought of the act gave me more focus, and oddly, more direction than I'd had in the weeks since my parents were killed.

"Oh well," I sighed as I looked down at Bounder's big shaggy head. I felt as bad for him as I did for myself. Listlessly, I gave his head a pat. He licked my hand in gratitude for this slight bit of recognition.

Suddenly I was aware of a horrendous noise growing louder by the second and then I felt something heavy hit me. I fell forward with a jolt; my face landed in the dust and dirt at the side of the road under the mailbox.

Dazed, I shook myself. "What in God's name happened?" I wondered aloud. I saw Bounder as he took a tentative step toward me then stopped. My attention was then drawn to the flickering brake lights of a speeding vehicle as it rounded the bend and roared off.

"Come, Bounder," I said softly, encouraging him to take another step. Something seemed wrong with the way he looked up at me.

"Bounder, Bounder," I whispered loudly as it dawned on me that the dog had just saved my life. "How had he known that we'd been in danger?"

At this instant, I was glad to be alive. Perhaps my meaningless life was not as worthless as I'd come to believe ....

"Oh, Bounder, you great, wonderful old thing, you!" I enthused as I felt him nudge up against me. He leaned on my leg and I couldn't help notice his weight and the warmth of him.

"Bounder," I said, my voice just now returning to normal. "It's okay. Let's get the mail and I'll give you a big treat when we get back to the house!"

I was reaching to get the mail and wondering what kind

of a treat would be good enough to show my appreciation for what he'd done when I became aware that his weight had increased tenfold.

"What the..." I gasped as I looked at Bounder and watched him slide down my leg to lie partly on my foot and partly in the dirt under the mail box.

"Bounder," I spoke louder and more sharply than I meant. On hearing his name and the panic in my voice, he attempted to get up and promptly fell back into the dust. I jumped back involuntarily trying not to get caught under his ninety-five pounds of dead weight. Upset and off balance, I tripped and ended up beside him.

"Bounder," I whispered as I reached for him. This time, he did not respond, did not move. I shook him slightly. I stared into his sightless eyes, caressed the dear grey face. I shuddered as I noticed that his tongue, fully extended, was lying in the dirt. I cried great wracking sobs. My only friend left in the world had just saved my life...and died.

I reached up to brush the tears from my eyes. As soon as I swept them away, my eyes flushed anew. I thought I'd never cry again after my parents' accident. I had carried a towel around with me for a week then—and knew I had wept every tear I would ever have in this life....

I cried now for Bounder, for life's ongoing cruelty and because I knew for sure that his life was over. At this point, I really had nothing to live for....

CHAPTER TWO

Every inch of me hurt. There was no escape in my memories as they either didn't exist or were too unpleasant to think about. I had no future—at least I had nothing to look forward to. My world was bleak, dark. I was unsure of everything.

I thought again of my past—what there was of it. Had I missed something? An important moment that might now give me purpose, something to hang on to, inspire me? I doubted it; but it was worth a try....

I went to the attic—hadn't been there for years. It was obviously my first trip since burying my parents. I was hesitant—afraid of what I might find there. However, I couldn't stop myself as I continued to slowly climb the stairs. I knew that my salvation was not going to be found here or anywhere, but I was drawn to it one step at a time, as metal to a magnet.

I'd existed for forty-one years and here I was with nothing to show for it.

"It's as though I've not lived, had no life," I reflected. In a sick way, the thought intrigued me—it was so hard to believe. Yet I knew it was true. It was my life I was talking about, after all. And I was being brutally honest about it. There wasn't any reason not to be. I had no one to impress.

Still, there was a time when I'd had a chance at life—my only opportunity as it turned out. But, of course, I didn't realize that at the time. Such is hindsight.

I thought back to that opportunity—the pivotal point in a relationship. I had once had a lover…not in the physical sense of the word. In those days 'nice girls didn't….' This man—I guess he was actually a boy—I'd known all my life. At 19 we fell in love—he deeply. I, being more than a little fickle, did not fall deeply but perhaps moderately, which was considerable for me in those early days.

We had a 'thing' for a couple of years. However, in time I found that I still sought a savior and the single life appealed to me more than any commitment of a romantic nature. After an off-and-on-again engagement, I had to make a decision, he said. I did. My decision was to get on with my life and not marry him. He went off to war.

I did not question my decision. In truth it was the only one I could have made at that particular time. But I did often wonder at my apparent inability to love deeply enough to make a sacrifice. I could have married him, sent him off happily to face his death in a rice paddy in Viet Nam. But no, I believe I hurt him deeply and then sent him off.

Fortunately, he did not die in the war and he did return sometime later and we made arrangements to meet. By then we'd both changed. He was now a man and I, a woman—still fickle, however. We no longer had the same feelings for one another and from the time we parted that day, we planned our lives and lived them independently. I believe he married and never looked back.

I, on the other hand, never married and have never stopped looking back. In the end, I saw him as my chance at life and happiness. I recognized the happiness that I passed up when I selfishly refused to marry him and sent him away to meet his fate. But as I said, I knew none of this at the time. I had only my then-thoughts and feelings to guide me and I'd acted accordingly. I did not know—could not know—that over the years, the fickle young girl would turn into an introverted old maid—one afraid to take chances and afraid to live life—for fear of making another mistake, perhaps?

Nor did I know that over the ensuing years subtle changes would take place and I would come to see that near-relationship as a missed opportunity, my only chance at real life. Looking back now, I realized that I had lived most of my life and experienced the little happiness I felt by dwelling in the past with my make-believe lover.

Funny, I now reflected grimly, that over time, with unerring focus, my mind had forgotten that I had totally lost my feelings for this man (as he for me). My mind, probably in its desperation to experience life, had replaced the real feelings of a dead relationship with passionate, loving, hopeful ones. My mind had resurrected, restored and protected the aborted love and that is what I lived with all these years. My mind apparently had known what I could not—that I would not have a life, never really know love and true passion.

Ironically, I had forfeited my chance, believing that the best was yet to come. I had been wrong and I knew that now. My life, I had to admit, was empty, barren, a veritable wasteland of dreams unfulfilled.

I shook my head sadly, as I took the last step up into the attic. I found my way to an old trunk with my parents' memories surrounding me. True, their lives were over, but they had been full, rich ones. They had lived and loved and been happy. In contrast, my life had never begun. I hung my head and cried for my lost life. Where did all these tears come from?

Much later, around dusk, I lifted my aching head and opened my red, puffy eyes. Without knowing why, I looked up at the ceiling and my attention was drawn to the beam carrying the electrical lines for the attic. Transfixed, I studied the frayed and ancient wires tacked there. I found myself focusing on one wire in particular. It left its counterparts and hung limply down. Once, there had been a bulb at its end; now it was a dangling wire.

I turned my eyes from it, but they were quickly drawn back. I found myself wondering if it were 'live.'

Without knowing why, I stood staring at it through fresh tears. I stepped toward that fascinating thing that held my attention so completely and would not let me go.

I breathed, "Lord, forgive me," and I reached up and grasped the dangling wire and squeezed it with all my might.

I felt, or imagined, a not unpleasant tingling sensation. I sighed and slipped to the floor, overwhelmed by the thoughts of what I had just done.

CHAPTER THREE

The next thing I knew I was in my room, standing in front of my old oak bureau. My jewelry box on top of the bureau lay open. I found myself staring at the antique brooch resting magnificently on the bright red velvet lining. The brilliance of the rubies, sapphires and diamonds fairly blinded me. The gems, all large and perfect cuts, glittered and shone although they had not been polished in years.

This brooch, a family heirloom and the single most valuable thing I owned, had been a gift to me from my parents on my twenty-first birthday. From that day, it had lain, like my life, protected from harm—safely locked away from any risks. The brooch, my mother had warned, was to be cherished, too valuable to actually be taken from its case and worn.

I stared at the brooch now and knew that it was symbolic of my life. My life also had been too valuable—too valuable to live, to actually take risks with....

After my one chance at love, I had slowly, unwittingly allowed myself to be protected from living. In the process, twenty-odd years had passed and though I'd been content living and working with my parents on our large, mid-western truck farm, I had effectively freed myself from the business of living. Even my relatively brief stint at a small college in the east was lost and unable to save me from myself and my eventual fate.

I shook my head sadly. "I am an empty vessel, a forty-one-year old virgin."

I glanced from the beautiful brooch to my reflection in the mirror above the oak bureau. Those eyes, were they my eyes looking back at me—seeing for the first time in perhaps two decades? Involuntarily, I took a step back. It seemed as though a stranger was looking at me from my mirror!

Those eyes could not belong to me, I thought in disbelief. Yet, I knew they did. I stared at them a long, long time and eventually I could see that they were indeed mine. They were so very different now!

Now they belonged to the reinvented me. "Yes," I breathed excitedly, "the all-new, much-improved me!"

Suddenly, I felt liberated and very anxious to make up for all those years of lost living. I knew what I was going to do about this travesty I'd allowed. I knew how I was going to go about this monumental task of creating a life for myself at this late date. With a still-trembling hand, I reached for the brooch and lifted it from its long-time resting place. I was amazed at its weight and balance. I pinned it to my worn sweatshirt.

I saw my reflection in the mirror and laughed aloud at the ridiculous combination—the elegant jewelry and the ratty, old sweatshirt.

"God," I mused, surprised at the sound of laughter. I wondered just how long it had been since I'd indulged myself. I asked myself where the laugh had come from, where it had been all these years? I wondered why I'd allowed my flame to be extinguished and the light of laughter banished from my all too-gloomy existence.

"How sad," I said to myself when I realized how very much I'd missed these long years. I was one who always loved to laugh, yet it had been ages since I had.

"Well," I said to myself as I carried on a conversation with my reflection in the mirror. "Things are going to be different from now on, I promise you, my girl," I spoke, sincerely to the face in the mirror.

"You have much to make up for...and make up for it you will!" I winked at myself and moved closer to the mirror. It was as though I was seeing myself for the very first time and I gasped. It was not a girl who looked back at me but a woman—and a middle-aged woman at that!

Where had the girl gone? When had I changed? How could I have become this person without even knowing it? I asked myself in disappointment, confusion and shock.

I peered closer, actually so close that my breath began to obscure my facial features. "Mercy," I breathed with relief as I looked at the cloudy vision before me.

Then, with a great deal of determination, I whipped some tissues from the Kleenex box on my bureau and hastily wiped at the fogginess to reveal what lay beneath.

Hmmm, I thought. Then said to myself, "Now let's see—just what do we have here?" I stared objectively at the face before me. I studied the small wrinkles on my forehead, my eyes still betraying the puffiness and redness of hours of tears. I saw little lines at the corners of my mouth that turned slightly downward.

Are those crow's feet? I gently touched the edge of my sore eyes and tried to pull the skin in a direction that would improve what I was seeing. It didn't work. I cursed under my breath—astounded at what my inventory revealed. I forced myself to continue.

"Glutton for punishment," I mumbled to the stranger in the mirror. I took in the small, red blotch on the side of my nose near the bridge, other lines, vertical ones this time at the side of my mouth. *Certainly not laugh lines*, I thought with some measure of cynicism.

"Ahhhh," I sucked my breath in as my eyes noticed the second chin for the first time. "God, this is painful!"

I swept my hair back between my two hands. I noticed my face did look a little like the old me when I applied some pressure and pulled the hair taut. I also noticed the many grey hairs, unnoticed until now, that framed my face above my ears. "And what in hell are these things?" I asked in horror as I saw these wiry, grey hairs about an inch or two long that sprang at will from the once-beautiful auburn hair.

Instantly, I let go of the hair I still held between my hands. It fell into place concealing the awful grey things.

"What nasty little tricks Mother Nature plays on us unsuspecting mortals," I huffed indignantly.

With purpose, I whirled around on the heel of one foot and strode to my closet. With false bravery I opened the door and stood before the full-length mirror on its inside panel. I stepped before it. *I might as well see what else has been going on while life was passing me by*, I thought glumly.

"Oh, no!" I shrieked, as a full-figured woman was reflected in the glass. *Circus mirror...* I thought without humor as I studied the large, shapeless form in front of me.

When had I lost the curves? Where had those extra pounds come from? When had gravity taken its toll and lowered those once-pert bosoms and those chins?

Suddenly, I knew it was going to be damned important to develop a sense of humor about all this and a steel-belted philosophy. Thoughtfully, I closed the closet door and walked over to my bed. I sat down with a thud. Once again I gave in to my overwrought emotions and I cried.

Gone were my thoughts to keep a sense of humor and to maintain a workable philosophy in the face of aging. I had lost so much more than my youth! I'd lost whatever looks I might have once had.

I wondered, *Could I get myself somewhat back in shape? Would it be possible to return a semblance of the attractiveness that was once attributed to me?* "Would it take a great deal of magic?" I asked aloud, brightening a little despite the repeated shocks of the last forty-five minutes' revelations. So much for the humor.

I asked myself weakly, "Is it really true that beauty comes from within?" That did it for the philosophy....

Sitting there, feeling the way I did, I decided I was going to have to get stern with myself. If my plan was going to work, I'd have to stop feeling sorry for myself and whip this old thing back into some shape or I'd get nowhere. I resolved to put the sniveling, sorry old woman away and let the new me run things from now on. I had a lot to do—a trip to plan—a lifetime of living to do in the next twelve months!

Briefly, I allowed myself to wonder how successful I'd be in fitting my life into the year ahead. After all, I'd been a 'child of the sixties' and gone to college and even worked for a short time in the East, yet I'd missed all the excitement everyone else of my era seemed to experience. I didn't get to Woodstock, or Haight-Ashbury either for that matter....

Quickly, I banished those thoughts and the ones I was beginning to have about William and my almost life.

I willed myself to concentrate on living and my plan for accomplishing this in a relatively short period of time. I knew I would go where I would, do what I would, and the more dangerous and exciting something was the more determined I was to experience it!

This then, was my plan, and the next year, if I lived that long, was my life. I was going to make it count! I couldn't wait to get started. I felt alive for the first time in decades. *Ironic*, I thought, *that I feel alive when I am more or less planning my death.* In throwing caution to the wind, I would live life to the fullest, but my life was likely to be forfeit in the encounter.

I didn't care! I had nothing to show for all these years but a mole or two and some curly, grey chicken-wire hairs... and oodles of regret. *Well, that was that.* The past was over and done with and now I'd live for the future. Even though it might not last too long, I just knew it would be worth it.

CHAPTER FOUR

I thought no more of my past or what I'd attempted to do with the dangling wire. Over the next few days I threw myself into house cleaning with all the abandon of a frustrated old maid, which I was now...however, for how much longer I did not know. I had rather high hopes for this great adventure of mine.

"Evangaline Hinton Moore is alive!" I declared with vim.

I mopped and scrubbed and cleaned the old house as a sergeant preparing for inspection by a tyrant of a general—a career-dependent inspection.

Since the house had always been well-cared for and cleaned constantly by me and my mother, it was shining in no time. I put away the mops and rags and gave a critical eye to the old homestead, 'Lazy Acres.' While surveying the product of several generations of Moores, I almost changed my mind about selling the place. *How could I do this to my parents' memory, my ancestors? What kind of person takes a one-way trip by selling her heritage?*

"Evangaline Hinton Moore, that's who!" I exclaimed as I gingerly picked up the receiver of the telephone and began to dial my one sort-of friend, a real estate agent.

I wasn't going to draw this worthless existence out and I didn't intend on staying here. I also knew I would not need a house because this would be my last trip. My last days on earth would be spent who knew where? All I knew was that it would not be here and I would not be returning.

I listened to the phone ring...once, twice. I nearly hung up.

"Hello," the voice on the other end, my sort-of friend, answered on the third ring. She said something else, but it was lost to me. I was too busy thinking out my plans.

"Hello," came the voice again, this time with a slight edge of annoyance to it. That brought me back to reality. If I was going to live, I had a house to sell.

"Hi, Ginny," I said brightly.

CHAPTER FIVE

It was done. I was free. Selling the house had been as easy as could be, yet it still seemed to take forever. But that was past and I now was beginning my adventure, my life.

I had a healthy amount of cash, traveler's checks, a credit card, a new wardrobe, a New York make-over, and, of course, my beloved brooch. I was ready to meet life head-on.

I'd never really drunk before but as I waited in the lounge at the airport, I sipped a CC and Ginger. I thought it was a very exciting drink! The gentleman who'd charmed the barmaid into opening the lounge early had ordered it for me. And, to my surprise, I liked it! He'd invited me to join him at the bar but I had much on my mind and preferred to savor the drink alone with my thoughts. I thanked him politely and moved myself and my drink to a quiet table in the corner.

As I waited for my flight from New York to Nassau, I sipped my mid-morning cocktail and thought I was off to a heck of a start. I was going to be in the Bahamas in a very short time. I reflected for just a moment about what I'd left behind in Ohio. Then I smiled—a genuine smile. My life was starting out pretty well, I had to admit. All the excitement and all the promise that should have been there, was.

I heard my flight called. I was on my way!

Reluctantly, I took one last sip and put my half-full drink on the table. I was so caught up in this heady adventure that I totally forgot about the kind gentleman who'd bought my first drink.

I struggled a little with my bags. I had a large purse, a couple of nondescript duffle-like bags and a roomy backpack from Marshall Fields that I'd purchased on a whim. I'd checked carefully to see that I could carry everything and even fit the duffels and my purse into the backpack, if necessary. I wanted only carry-on luggage and I wanted to be as compact and independent as possible.

My insides were aflutter and I felt giddy as I boarded my first plane in a couple of decades. I was frightened, or rather a little intimidated, at the boldness of the new me. But any reservations I had about selling the farm and taking this one-way trip were cancelled as I took my seat and felt the rush of being totally free and in charge of things.

I couldn't believe the power of the jet engines as my body was forced against the back of my seat during take-off. It was exhilarating and I was like a small child experiencing her first thrill in life. Even knowing that the most dangerous part of flying was the takeoff and first few minutes in the air did not diminish my excitement.

As we cruised the multi-colored blue skies high above the clouds, I pressed my hand to the brooch pinned inside my pantsuit jacket. I hadn't quite gotten to the point where I dared wear it exposed, but I wanted it near me. I patted it reassuringly,

"Excuse me, Miss," came a melodious voice.

Startled out of my reverie, I turned to see a smiling stewardess dropping my tray table in front of me. She placed a small bottle of Canadian Club and a plastic cup filled with ginger ale and ice on a napkin on the little tray.

Surprised, I started to ask where the drink had come from but she anticipated my question and said, "From the gentleman two seats behind you,"

I turned around to smile my thanks. The plane was not very crowded and most of the occupants sat alone in the row of seats. The gentleman who'd bought me my second CC & Ginger was the same man who'd bought my first in the airport lounge. He was engaged in conversation with a very attractive woman sitting behind him.

I shrugged and returned to my drink and the beautiful designs of the clouds we flew above. *Oh, my God,* I thought. *Whoever dreamed life could be this delicious?* I almost felt guilty as I sipped my drink and contemplated what this adventure would offer forth.

Before I finished my drink, another arrived. This time when I turned to thank the man who was supplying me with cocktails, I was surprised to see that his seat was empty.

If he's drinking as much as I am, he's probably in the bathroom, I thought and realized at the same time that I was beginning to get uncomfortable with a near-full bladder.

Oh, well, I thought, resigned to the awkward trip down the aisle to the lavatories at the rear of the plane. *Maybe I'll pass my benefactor and be able to thank him properly.*

The alcohol was taking effect, and I giggled a little at the prospect of running into him outside the bathrooms. I knew I'd probably be mortified. After all, he was a very handsome man, tall and lean with great green eyes and high cheekbones in a tanned face. He looked like my idea of an Adonis except that he had brown hair instead of blonde.

I hated to admit it, but his looks were so disarming I knew that was the real reason I'd not accepted his offer to join him at the lounge bar back at the airport.

"Hmm," I sighed, as I made my way down the aisle to the bathrooms. I checked one door then the other. Both had vacancy signs on them. "Odd," I mused, "where could he have gone to?"

I checked back to his seat and glanced quickly around the plane before stepping into the bathroom to relieve myself. He was nowhere in sight.

For a moment I thought maybe I'd made the fellow up, invented the whole scenario of the handsome stranger buying me drinks from New York to Nassau, but I knew, even with my over-sized imagination, that I had not.

I fussed with myself, trying to pink my cheeks by pinching them and straightening my clothes that were now beginning to show the effects of travel. The bathroom was so tiny that I had all I could do to turn around so I soon gave up trying to improve my appearance and headed back to my seat. There was a limit to what I could do under the best of conditions.

I noticed that the stranger's seat was still unoccupied but now there was a no-vacancy sign on the opposite bathroom door. I sighed, suddenly aware of the turbulence and the liquor sloshing around in my empty stomach. I made my way unsteadily back to my assigned seat and spent the duration of the trip alternating between euphoria and illness. I kept the air sickness bag clutched in my hand and prayed I would not need it. I could see that I was going to have to do a lot of field work before I was a seasoned traveler.

Well, I consoled myself, *you've certainly had a lot less pleasant assignments in life.* I would have chuckled at the irony of that had I not felt so nauseous.

Thankfully, we soon reached our destination. I had just enough time to look quickly out the window as the plane banked into a descending turn. Over the intercom, the captain pointed out a few atolls and gave the temperature and humidity on the island while I gasped at the sights below me.

The water seemed composed of every imaginable shade of green and blue. I could see the sandy beaches and the little fingers of sand that stretched seemingly endlessly into the ocean.

"Oh, my God," I breathed as the sight literally took my breath away. I saw dark objects in the water and wondered if they were sharks...or rocks, or what.

The sights just before landing were so breathtaking that I almost forgot I was ill; I remembered as soon as the plane's wheels touched down on the runway with a quick jerk.

Gathering all my resolve to have the time of my life, I got my luggage together, and with something akin to a lump in my throat, made my way along with the other deplaning passengers to customs. When I stepped out of the plane I was hit with the most intense blast of warmth I'd ever felt. "Oh," I said, unaware that I'd uttered a word,

"Yes, isn't it something?" came a voice behind me.

I turned to see the glowing face of a young college student, wearing the requisite school soccer t-shirt and cut-offs with sandals. I envied her beauty and youth and that figure.

"Beautiful," I agreed as someone tapped me on the shoulder and my attention was diverted to a Bahamian gentleman in brightly colored garb offering me a very exotic-looking pink drink. I stared at the little umbrella and all the bits of fruit in the drink and shook my head "no". Then, abruptly changing my mind, I quickly reached for the drink, catching him off guard.

"Why the hell not?" I said. "I'm here to live dangerously!"

The man seemed thrilled at my sudden change of heart and with a free hand he clapped me on the back. "Yes," he said, "I know you will love the Bahamas. I drive taxi in my spare time," he laughed. "I'll show you the islands as they should be seen and I promise you, you'll have the time of your life!"

I gulped the drink and took one last furtive look around for my gentleman friend on the plane. He was nowhere to be seen.

"Well," I giggled, feeling a lot better with each sip of this delicious whatever-it-was. "I think I just might take you up on that offer!"

"Wonderful," he boomed, and handed me a surprisingly tasteful business card. I gave him my best smile, took another long pull on the drink he'd given me as a welcome to the Bahamas and promised I'd call him when I got ready for my island tour.

I toddled off to customs, sucking on my pink drink and thinking I couldn't wait to hit the beautiful beaches I'd seen from the air.

"Oh, God," I thought as the customs inspector welcomed me to the island and began to ask questions. I was feeling much better and responded in kind to his teasing me about my drink and first trip to Nassau.

Before I knew it, I was stepping out of the terminal into the bright sunshine and I already had two dates lined up! The customs inspector was coming by my hotel later to take me for the best 'pink drink' on the island. I couldn't wait!

I stepped to the pavement and hailed a cab. By this time, I'd completely forgotten about the man from New York.

I pushed my bags into the backseat and climbed in beside them. I was already sweltering in my New York pantsuit. As I twisted out of the jacket, the cabbie turned to me and smiled, "Where to, my princess?"

I gave him the name of my hotel and couldn't help marveling at the friendliness of the Bahamians I'd met thus far. As the cab driver kept up a non-stop one-way conversation, I wondered if everyone here would be so friendly. It was incredible to me to be in a strange place and feel so very welcome.

The cab driver sped along the road, traveling so fast that he nearly frightened me to death when he narrowly missed another cab coming from the opposite direction. The almost-encounter didn't seem to faze him because he never paused for a breath in his monologue.

The windows of the cab were wide open and I could smell the sweet perfumes emanating from the exotic flowers that seemed to be everywhere I looked. I was already intoxicated by this island paradise—its alluring beauty, fabulous climate and friendly people. For a moment I almost abandoned my plan to travel around and live recklessly until the end.

Why not just stay here and kill myself with kindness and pink drinks? I thought as the taxi pulled to a halt outside my three-story pink stucco hotel. If I'd known what lay ahead on this trip, I'd have definitely given the matter more serious thought! As a matter of fact, I'd never have left Ohio.

"Ah, yes, my princess," the cabbie rambled on as he opened my door and pulled the bags from the seat beside me.

"You will love it here—just love it!"

He extended his hand graciously and with exaggerated ceremony helped me from the cab. Then he too gave me a card and told me to call on him if I needed any transportation during my stay in Nassau. He seemed not to have noticed that I'd totally ignored him during the ride to my hotel. He was as pleasant as he could be—making me feel slightly guilty that I hadn't paid any attention to him.

I paid my fare and included a generous tip, which encouraged him to repeat his offer to ferry me around should I so desire. "I buy you a drink, a fine 'Yellow Bird.' Yellow Bird's one of our specialties—we make the best in the world! You'll like it, you'll see. Call me," he said with a huge smile and friendly wave. He got back into his cab and sped away leaving me standing in front of my hotel with a big smile and feeling very much like a princess.

CHAPTER SIX

"Eeeeeee," I heard this drunken, gleeful squeal.

"What the ..." I said to myself as I stepped back off the sidewalk and into the street. "Eeeeeee," came the same noise as I looked up to the third balcony of the hotel where there were several young girls in various states of undress.

There on the balcony screeching with delight was the same coed in college T, cutoffs and sandals, who had been beside me in the customs line at the airport. She was now busy stirring a drink and laughing while yelling a challenge to unseen person or persons below her. The other girls hovered around her, egging her on,

"Wait, wait, not ready yet!" I heard a distinctive male voice scream from somewhere inside the second balcony.

The girls hooted in response.

Just then, several bare-chested young men in shower caps and swimming trunks materialized just below the third floor balcony. The girls disappeared inside their room and returned, each with a full glass.

I watched mesmerized as, in unison, the girls poured the

contents of their glasses into the open mouths waiting below.

Oh my, I thought, *no sleep if this is any example of what awaits me at this hotel.* Then I perked up a bit. *Hell,* I thought, *what on earth is wrong with me? I certainly did not come all the way to Nassau for sleep!*

"Hey! Hey, you!" came the voice from above. "Hi!" she said as she saw she'd caught my attention. It was the girl from the customs line. She threw something in my direction and yelled "C'mon up—join the fun!"

I looked down at my feet to where the room key she'd thrown me had landed. I couldn't help smiling.

"Why not?" I called and went into the hotel to register and make my way to my room. I'd change into something more suitable for tossing drinks off balconies and join the coed and her friends. I knew I could learn a lot from these girls and I really couldn't wait to get started!

As it happened, my room was on the same floor and right across from the girls. By the time I was unlocking my door, the hall was flooded with people, mostly young men responding to the taunting women on the balcony. I wondered if they were now dragging the men off the street to join them in their partying.

Again I thought, *Why not?*

I slipped into some pale yellow culottes and a white cotton top. I slid my feet into new sandals and went to the mirror to check my appearance. Compared to the girls next door there was no contest but, I contented myself, "Not half bad."

I'd managed to lose fifteen pounds before the house sold. Actually, it hadn't been all that hard since I was so busy running around and working on raw nerves with every prospective buyer. With the right clothes, it seemed to make a real difference in my overall appearance. I didn't look as old and dowdy as I had when I'd first taken note of myself after all those years of indifference or whatever had caused me to neglect my physical appearance.

But, I thought with brutal honesty, *I could still lose more weight.* "Right," I said to my face in the mirror. "Well, too bad, as the saying goes, 'I'm not here for a long time—just a good time'!"

I was going to have a good time for sure. And I wasn't going to make myself miserable by making comparisons, I continued to lecture myself.

Suddenly the din next door was unbelievably loud. I stepped onto my own balcony, next to the girls', and watched in awe as these women struck up screaming matches with the young male passers-by on the sidewalk below.

"Hey, aren't you coming over? You're missing all the fun!"

I looked across to see the girl from the customs line.

"I am indeed—be right there!" I hollered. Quickly, I re-entered my room, picked up the key thrown to me before I checked in and headed across the hallway to where the party was quickly getting out of hand.

When I was just inside the door, doing my best to locate the coed and return her key, I was pushed into a man of about my age—something I surely hadn't expected with this bunch!

He turned to me and said, "Well, well, well...." He paused and looked at me intently for a moment. "I can't believe my charges had the good sense to draft you to their den of iniquity," and he smiled a most beguiling smile.

I gave him the same serious assessment he'd given me a moment before. He was, as I said, about my age, very handsome with curly light grey hair that almost looked sandy in color. His eyes were a light blue with greenish flecks on the outer side of the iris. Long lashes blessed those fantastic eyes. He had a slightly ruddy complexion and the sleek build of an athlete. He was wearing loose-fitting khaki shorts and a short sleeved, white button-down shirt. He had well-worn moccasins on his feet. I sensed this was a real man and my face felt hot and, I suspected, instantly colored.

Slightly taken aback by my reaction to this man, I simply said, "I beg your pardon," took a step back and smiled my most winning smile. I hoped he would not detect my rather obvious attraction to him.

"Oh, I'm sorry," he said easily and extended his hand.

"I'm Bill Tanner. I'm one of the chaperones for this group of unruly students. We're from a small college in New Hampshire—here for 10 days' spring break, if we survive it.... Would you believe we only checked in an hour ago?"

He smiled at me.

I had to strain to stay within arm's length of him. People were pushing and shoving as bodies tried to get in and out of the room.

"One minute," he said. "I'm going to attempt to bring some order to this chaos."

I jumped to the most piercing whistle I'd ever heard. Amazingly, the noise quieted several decimals.

In a loud, authoritative but not angry voice, Bill Tanner spoke to the people in the room and out on the side and front balconies.

"Hey, quiet down, kids, I'd hate to have us thrown out of our hotel and spend the rest of our break on the beach. I'm sure you'll agree if you take the time to think about it.

"So, let's have only members of our group in the room

now. The rest of you will have to return to wherever you came from. I'm sure we'll be seeing each other around in the next week or so."

He smiled graciously as one-by-one the newcomers filed out the door.

I looked for the girl who'd tossed me her key and spotted her at the makeshift bar, fixing herself and someone else a drink, "There you are," I said, walking up to her and discreetly slipping her the key.

"Lexy," she grinned. "Alexis Morris at your service." She handed the second drink to me and lifted her glass in a toast.

"Cheers!"

I took a sip and it was delicious.

"Thank you," I said. "But, I've really got to be getting back to my room. I haven't even unpacked and I still want to spend some time on the beach."

I felt a hand on my shoulder and turned to see Bill Tanner. He started to speak but Lexy was already apologizing for inviting all those people to her room.

"Dr. Tanner, I'm sorry. I didn't mean to get so carried away. I'll try not to let it happen again."

"Of course, Alexis, I'm sure that you will," he said and winked slyly at me. I grinned. "Now, if you'll excuse me, I'd like to get better acquainted with this young lady here," he said gesturing to me.

Lexy, drink in hand, was skipping to the door. "I'll see you soon," she waved to me and disappeared through the door. The room was suddenly quiet. I looked around. It was empty except for Dr. Tanner and me.

"My goodness," I couldn't help uttering. "Where did everyone disappear to?" I was astonished at how quickly everyone had vanished, and I was once again aware of the effect Bill Tanner's nearness had on me. I was embarrassed and made a lame excuse to return to my room and unpack.

"Great!" he said, "I'll be by, say fifteen minutes, and we can get some sun if you don't mind?"

Mind, I thought, *I'd love it!* But instead, I said "Sure, that will be fine."

CHAPTER SEVEN

The next several days were a whirlwind of activity. Somehow I did manage to make my tour of the island with the part-time cab driver I'd made a date with at the airport. I learned all sorts of interesting things about the Bahamian culture and drank some of the most wonderful concoctions of liquor and fruit in the world! In between stops at the 'best' clubs on the island, I was entertained with local stories and found this man to be fascinating and witty. The evening was fabulous—even though I'd turned down a date with the drop-dead handsome Dr. Tanner to keep my previous commitment. I was surprised to find that at the end of the night, I was not sorry.

I met and spent time with many of the college students as well as Bill Tanner. We occasionally went to the beach, but most of the time we found ourselves in various bars enjoying the island specialty drinks. I spent the majority of my time in some level of intoxication and thought it was just the most delightful state.

As time wore on, I found myself spending less and less time at the beach and sleeping in so that I could howl half the night with my new-found friends. I'd probably be the only person leaving the island without a tan! I found myself wondering why I hadn't gone on a trip like this when I was Lexy's age. I'd had the opportunity when I was in college and had not been interested at the time.

"No fool like an old fool," I smiled, forgiving myself for the error of twenty-odd years ago. I certainly would make up for it now. I giggled to myself. I was having such a wonderful time! And, I had to admit, the tan wouldn't amount to much in the end. But these memories would be my life for as long as it lasted.

Off and on in my more sober moments, I thought about the stranger I'd dubbed "The CC and Gingerman." For some reason I couldn't quite get him out of my mind...even with the near-constant attention of Dr. Tanner. I enjoyed Bill's company, as well as that of his fellow chaperones, but Bill did not excite me physically once I got to know him.

Bill was an excellent companion, full of interesting stories about his past adventures in Nassau. He and the other two chaperones with him had been taking students from their college on this Nassau trip for the past seven years. Although the students changed from year to year, the fun and Island's allure did not. As a result of his many trips, he knew all the great watering holes and had made some Bahamian friends that he kept in touch with throughout the year.

Bill and the other two chaperones—Hilly, short for Hildegarde, and Mary—took me 'over the hill' into the native section of Nassau and treated me to some real island entertainment at the Drum Beat Club. The place was so wild and the dancing so suggestive that I told Bill I'd be embarrassed to death for the students to see me acting quite this uninhibited.

He turned and smiled at me. "Well, my dear, you really don't have a thing to worry about in that department." He drew a circle with a wave of his hand indicating Mary and Hilly.

"Our charges are not allowed over here. As a matter of fact, they are not allowed in the native areas at all, and specifically not in the Drum Beat Club. I wouldn't come myself if I didn't have friends behind the bar and at the door here."

"Oh, I see." I had yet to meet any of his island friends. But I guessed tonight I would. I just hoped I'd be sober enough to remember them.

"Yes," Bill continued. "Tonight is all ours. We," again indicating his fellow chaperones, "can live it up and the kids will be none the wiser. At least, we have the freedom to act as we want without those young eyes taking everything in."

I didn't think Mary and Hilly were paying particular attention to what Bill was saying. They were gyrating in place to the music, laughing and smiling, and occasionally waving to people as they stood next to us. But as soon as Bill finished speaking, they nodded and grinned their agreement. It was obvious that this trip to the Drum Beat Club was a favorite of the chaperones and that they really did let their hair down without fear of being discovered by their students.

I knew I was in for a treat and I was not disappointed. As dawn approached, Bill and I staggered to our little bamboo table, exhausted and sweating from all the frenzied dancing we'd done. Suddenly there was a tap on my shoulder and I turned around to look straight into the laughing face of Lexy!

"Fancy running into you here!" she slurred.

I looked at Bill for a reaction. He did his best to collect himself and address the situation, but it was quite clear that

in all the years he'd chaperoned these trips, he had never met
the likes of Lexy. She had no regard for authority, loved life
and knew how to live it at an early age. How I envied her
philosophy… but not her current problems.

Bill was so angry that he actually looked purple in the
eerie lantern light.

"Excuse us," he said, biting off each word and using all
his self-control to not say more until he had Lexy off where
they could have a private conversation.

I barely heard, "And who else from our group is here?
How did you get here? Where is your escort?"

Then the music started up again and any further
admonishments were drowned out by the pulsing drum beat.

I knew it could be dangerous to go into the native areas
unescorted. I couldn't tell whether Bill was more concerned
for her safety or angry at the fact she'd directly gone against
one of the few rules the group had—or if he was upset that
he and his fellow teachers had lost their one safe haven—the
one place they could be themselves without being responsible
for others.

When I thought about Mary and Hilly, I started to look
for them. Actually, I was beginning to feel a little vulnerable in
the midst of all these twisting booze-fueled bodies. I couldn't
locate the female chaperones and I couldn't find the two men
I'd met earlier, Bahamians that Bill counted as friends and
had known for years. I did spot Columbus, another of Bill's
friends, who was frantically mixing drinks behind the bar.
Although not at ease, I felt better that there was at least one
person with whom I was acquainted. I made my way slowly
and carefully toward the bar.

Even though I hadn't experienced any hostility from
the native Bahamians here at the club, I had not forgotten

the little unpleasant incidents that had begun to occur more and more frequently the longer we stayed in Nassau. The first example of friction between whites and blacks that I witnessed happened on the beach my second day in Nassau. A little group of young black children, all boys, kept sneaking up on the college girls who were trying to sun themselves. The boys would grab the inevitable tube of suntan lotion and begin to massage the coeds. Needless to say, the girls were uncomfortable with this kind of harassment and soon found other places to spend their time. The boys didn't really do any harm but they did manage to create a feeling of unease. They quickly made the hotel beach an uncomfortable place to work on one's tan. Since it was mainly a tourist beach, it soon became virtually deserted.

Also, there were increasing reports of young black men grabbing the crotches and busts of female tourists walking alone. The men would pat the women's breasts or derrieres and then keep on walking as though nothing had happened. Again, this open antagonism had the desired effect. Girls were warned to go nowhere alone, not even to the shopping areas, as these were the places where the aggression frequently occurred.

This situation was a first for Bill and his seasoned chaperones. It was a strange thing that we'd all have to be aware of and be very cautious about until after the election. I hadn't thought much about it when Bill explained it to me on one of our nights of barhopping shortly after we met. Also, though I knew little about the island, I had to agree with Bill when he said, "You know, in the final analysis, I'm not sure any tourist could really understand what's at stake, the feelings, the situation here. I expect only the Bahamian people themselves can truly appreciate how they feel."

For some reason I was thinking about it now. All of a sudden, I felt very much the minority and very vulnerable. I had a vision of the whole place turning on me, beating me with their fists until I fell to the floor and then violently suffocating me to death. It was a quick and fleeting impression that came at me from out of the blue but it caused me to experience a sudden chill. I doubled my effort to get to the part of the bar where Columbus was still madly mixing drinks. I glanced around as I zeroed in on my destination, nowhere could I see Bill and Lexy or Mary and Hilly.

The temperature was probably in the eighties but I had goose bumps and could not stop shivering. I kept wondering about the next 'incident.' What if someone was really hurt—or killed. Things seemed to be heading in the more violent direction. I pressed forward with increased purpose.

I felt much better when I found a seat in front of Columbus' bar station and he smiled warmly at me. His grin reassured me somewhat and I began to relax. I watched in fascination as he whipped up drink after drink—each one seemingly more complicated than the last. He certainly was an impressive bartender! After only a week in Nassau, I felt qualified to assess such things. My education was expanding—even if not in the best or most impressive of directions.

I'd almost forgotten about my earlier concerns when I felt someone staring at me. As casually as I could, I turned the old wooden barstool toward the corner of the club. I damn near died when I saw my CC and Gingerman staring at me from some distance. When he saw he'd caught my eye, he waved and beckoned me to him. Despite my inhibitions, well-worn at this point of the night, I fairly leapt off my seat and without a second thought, headed in his direction.

My legs felt wobbly and unreliable. I experienced a rush of heat to my neck and face—incredibly I was excited at the thought of talking to this man. I was blushing! This time, my dizziness was not due to the alcohol I'd consumed but rather to the intoxicating effect of the stranger I'd first seen in the New York bar lounge seven days ago.

Where had he disappeared to on the plane? Where had he been all this time in Nassau? All the times my new-found friends and I had barhopped or walked arm-in-arm down the street warbling *We all live in a yellow submarine, yellow submarine...*, I'd nary a glimpse of him. And with the exception of Paradise Island where I'd only been twice during the past week, I thought I'd really been around. *What was he doing here?*

"Hello," he said as I approached him and he took my hand in his. "I was wondering when I'd have a chance to finally spend some time with you. It looks as though this is my lucky night."

I gulped, hardly believing my ears. I swallowed again, frantically trying to think of a proper response to that remark.

"Oh there you are," Bill barged right in between us, breaking the Gingerman's grip on me. "I'm sorry," he apologized, "but we must leave now." There was no missing the finality, the anxiety in his voice.

"But, but...." I stammered.

"No *buts*," Bill said sternly as he grabbed my arm and almost dragged me through the crowd to a taxi waiting outside. Therein sat Lexy, Mary and Hilly, all looking miserable.

I didn't understand what was going on. Was it Lexy's arrival that so upset Bill or was there something else he feared?

Despite the possible danger of remaining, I desperately wanted to stay and talk with the Gingerman. One look at Bill and the group in the cab convinced me not to press the issue. Reluctantly, I squeezed into the back seat with Mary and Hilly. Bill climbed in front with Lexy and as soon as we were settled, the cab sped off. For some reason I felt as though I'd left my best friend behind—imagine, a man I didn't even know!

I was definitely changing. The spinster who'd left Ohio a short time ago was falling away to something new, *infinitely more interesting*, I thought. I was living now, not merely existing. I found I was even relishing the disappointments. Perhaps it was because I had hopes that this last one—the almost meaningful encounter—would eventually turn out differently. Something told me that if I got a second chance, it would be well worth the wait. The fact that I might appear somewhat in demand and elusive to the Gingerman could heighten my own appeal to him.

I smiled. I had learned much by watching the wily Lexy and quizzing her about the opposite sex. For one so young, she was long on strategy. I don't remember a longer cab ride than the one we took from the Drum Beat Club to our hotel. It was obvious that something was bothering Bill. He was silent for the first few minutes; then he spoke mostly to Lexy—I assumed since Mary, Hilly and I had already been told of the underlying problem in Nassau this trip.

Bill spoke in a low, controlled voice.

"As you know, Nassau, actually the Bahamas, is a British protectorate and has the same form of government as their motherland. They have political parties, mainly the UBP—United Bahamian Party, consisting of the black population, and the PLP—the Peoples' Liberation Party—is its white counterpart. One of the white members has recently died and there will soon be an election to determine his successor. The candidate who wins the election will have the majority vote and rule the island. I understand that the blacks have not been in control of the government for over 100 years and this is their first shot at it. Unfortunately, this makes for a very tense situation on the island and has basically pitted black against white. The closer the election draws, the more tension and violent acts are happening. I'm very concerned for the safety of our group—I'm even thinking of canceling the rest of the trip and leaving the island.

"I heard something inside the club, actually one of my friends told me. I'm not going to repeat what he said as he asked me not to, but there is a definite and concerted effort on the part of some of the more radical Blacks and they are looking to create serious problems. My friend is afraid that the most vulnerable group is the tourists, and the college kids, in particular, make a perfect target.

"As soon as we get back to the hotel; I'm going to see if I can move our departure up. If not, I will be going to all the male rooms and Mary and Hilly will visit each of the girls' rooms and issue some specific rules regarding the remainder of our stay here."

He cleared his throat and continued. "I'm very sorry but I would never have taken this trip if I'd known what was going on here. I have a feeling we're in danger and I won't get over it until I have everyone safe and sound on the plane out of here.

Mary, Hilly and I exchanged glances with each other and Lexy. Lexy looked momentarily chastened but we all knew it wouldn't take her long to bounce back to her normal, exuberant self.

Later, I had trouble falling asleep. I thought not about my missed opportunity with the Gingerman but the possibility I'd not be able to spend the next few days with my friends. I'd grown fond of them and I'd hoped to enjoy the pleasure of their company for the next three days. Now that there was a chance they'd be leaving tomorrow, I knew I would miss them a great deal. I had no idea what I'd do with myself after they'd gone.

CHAPTER EIGHT

The next day dawned as perfect as the last seven. The weather was absolutely heavenly in this part of the world. I dragged myself from bed, threw on a light cotton robe and stepped out on my front balcony to glimpse the shimmering sea. I watched in fascination as the sun danced on the slightly rippling water. For a moment I thought I was looking at a field of diamonds instead of tiny waves washing to shore.

Thinking of diamonds made me think of my brooch. God! I'd been so busy with my new social life that I'd totally forgotten about it. I hadn't checked it for the week that I'd been in Nassau. I shook my head in disgust—if I had lost it, it was my own damned fault. I hadn't taken the time to put it in the hotel vault, though I meant to, of course—*or had I?*

I went over to the duffel I'd put it in. I was half afraid of what I'd find. I carefully searched the little compartment inside the bag and found the sanitary napkin I'd stuffed it in. To my relief, the brooch was still there and just as beautiful as ever. I looked at it for a moment and then put it away.

Just then my attention was drawn to a piece of lined

paper folded in half and lying under my door. I took a step toward it and could see that it was notebook paper. It was from Bill. I didn't realize that I was holding my breath as I quickly unfolded the paper.

"Hilly and I will pick you up at ten for breakfast, then we'll head to Paradise Island. We'll fill you in then. Yours, Bill."

I let out a great sigh of relief. I'd have my friends around longer, even if it were for just one more day. Suddenly I had energy. My sleepless night was all but forgotten as I laid a white and pale pink sundress on my bed and headed for the shower to freshen up. Bill and Hilly arrived shortly before ten but I was ready to go and excited as hell.

Swearing, I thought. *Another thing I'd picked up from Lexy.* I smiled. Bill, Hilly and I made our way to Lum's for breakfast, which included our usual pitchers of beer. We spoke very little until we'd been seated and ordered; then Bill spoke.

"Well, I'm sure you've gathered that we couldn't change our reservations."

I nodded, trying not to show how happy that made me. I knew I was being selfish. Bill had the responsibility of the group's safety and he was obligated to do what was necessary to protect his charges. I could see that he wasn't happy about the reservations but he appeared to be attempting to make the best of it. He wasn't doing a very good job. "Mary is staying in the hotel today. We'll take turns so that one of us is there at all times in case there's trouble and we're needed.

"Last night we had a meeting and made that decision. We also decided that the kids should spend as much time as possible in and around the hotel. If they go out, it's to be in groups and with the chaperones' knowledge of destination, expected time of return, etc. The only place we've authorized them to go is Paradise Island. There are mostly tourists there—no natives except employees who value their jobs and wouldn't be likely to jeopardize them. They are to take cabs to and from...no beaches...midnight curfew. Well, you get the idea.

"After that meeting, we split up and went to each room and made the situation crystal clear to the kids. It was a long night to say the least." Bill yawned then smiled wanly. "The students don't feel quite the same as we adults do. Youth—they think they're invincible.

"I hated to put such a damper on this trip, especially when we've had such a good time up 'til now. I think they now feel like our prisoners, but really," he explained, "I'm doing it for their own good."

"Well," I smiled. "I don't think being confined to the casinos and beaches and bars at Paradise Island is such a bad sentence!"

"You're right," Hilly agreed, catching my effort to lighten the mood. "Yes, let's make the best of our remaining time in Nassau!"

"Hear, hear!" Bill raised his mug of beer and Hilly and I said, "Hear, hear!" in unison. We laughed in relief as we all toasted our commitment to making the best of a bad situation. The underlying tension on the island had us all affected. Until this discussion, I'm not sure we were fully aware of that, but it was evident now.

We made small talk, laughed together at some of the stories about the students' hijinks and finished the remainder of our pitchers.

By the time we hailed a cab, we were in a much better frame of mind. As the taxi passed over the causeway separating Nassau proper from Paradise Island, we breathed a collective sigh of relief. The transition was complete and we felt like carefree tourists once again.

During the course of the day we ran into most of the group. It seemed by their actions and demeanors that they weren't taking this imposed sentence too hard. They ate, drank, gambled, teased one another and generally acted like kids letting off steam and celebrating. They were in a tropical paradise and after a long New England winter and semester exams, they were making the most of their time— not overly concerned, apparently, with the heat and fire of island politics run amok. And that pleased Bill and Hilly.

I was glad for the chaperones. Although I had no responsibility for the group, I so closely identified with them that their concerns felt like my own.

At one point, Hilly and I were sitting at a table together chatting. Bill was playing blackjack and had managed to win a few hands.

"You know, Evie, I think Bill has a thing for you," Hilly smiled expectantly.

I didn't know what to say so I took another sip of my 'pink drink,' as I had come to call those lethal concoctions of rums and fruit juices.

"Well, most women would give their right arms for a tumble with him, Evie. Do you know half the single women in town have chased after him—not to mention the available," and she cleared her throat, "and some not-so-available faculty members...."

"Yes, I'm not surprised, Hilly. Bill is a handsome man. He's absolutely wonderful, sweet, considerate...." I wasn't sure where I was going with this response.

"But," Hilly supplied.

"But, aside from an initial rather impressive reaction to

his presence, I don't have any interest in a relationship—other than platonic," I added quickly.

"It's hard to explain it to you. I think of him like I think of you and Mary—friends, dear friends—even though we've known each other for such a short time.

"Anyway, to answer your question...."

Hilly interrupted, "You already have, I think...you're really something special, you are...," she said and leaned toward me and gave me a spontaneous hug.

"I'm fond of you all," I supplied lamely. But her compliment was not lost on me. Maybe I was developing an identity, a personality that others found attractive. I knew that I was proud of myself.

Early on, when I had reached for the dangling wire and made my decision to take this trip and continue to reach for it in every action, I'd wondered about the effect men would have on me. More to the point, I wondered if I'd have any opportunities with them and if I'd be man-crazy after all those years of celibacy and isolation in Ohio. I felt I'd passed my first test.

I gave Hilly my best and brightest smile, which the pink drinks only intensified. I held my drink up to hers: "To friends."

"To *dear* friends," Hilly corrected me and we clicked glasses in agreement.

"What's all this?" Bill asked as he strode to the table.

"Bonding," Hilly answered and gave me a conspiratorial wink.

"Ah," Bill said, knowing the wisest course was to get on to the next topic.

"What do you ladies say to something to eat, then hitting the beach for an hour or so?"

"Fine with me," I smiled,

"Me too," said Hilly.

"Good, it's settled. Where do you want to dine?"

"I don't care. Let's wander around and see what appeals to us. There's just so much to offer here and so many famous faces that it's a bit too much to absorb in such a short time," Hilly said with an exaggerated lilt in her imitation southern drawl. She batted her long lashes for added effect.

"Oh, Hilly," Bill laughed, "you look like you're taking it all in stride. After all, you've been here before and you don't fool us for a minute. Overwhelmed, my eye!" Bill exclaimed and grabbed us each by an elbow and escorted us out of the main casino.

From that point on, I can't really remember what we did except have a wonderful time. It seems that we lost track of time because it was one a.m. when we called for a cab and nobody had intended on staying out that late.

Mary was on the sidewalk in front of the hotel when our cab pulled up. She was frantic, fairly pulling Bill out of the passenger seat.

"Bill, Bill, it's Lexy. She's not back and we can't find her. She's late, Bill—well over an hour late and I'm sick with worry. I know something's happened to her. I just know it. She didn't call. She..."

"Calm down, Mary. Easy. Now, tell me what you know, where you looked. Did you talk with the other students? Where was the last place she was seen? By whom? Who was she with?" He fired the questions at Mary as he hustled her inside.

Hilly and I followed them inside, too sick with fear to speak. Suddenly the pervasive feeling of danger was back with a vengeance. I had no doubt that something terrible had happened to Alexis. I couldn't explain it; my gut just knew it.

I tried to keep my panic to myself as I followed the questions and answers regarding Lexy.

"I did the room check after curfew," Mary said, fighting for control of her emotions. "Everyone was in their rooms except Bob Martin and Sandy Weitz but they came in while I was still taking headcount. Then I got to Lexy's room. Her roommates hadn't seen her since noon. She was here in the hotel hanging around with that young fellow she's been seeing down here."

"Which young fellow? She's had several...ah, admirers...."

"The older guy, the meat inspector with the government. You know the one that's been here several times before—I thought we'd met him briefly in the past. You know, comes with another inspector, his buddy since childhood or something like that. The nice looking blonde man, tall...not his friend, the one we spoke with just yesterday. He and Lexy were in the lobby together when we were on our way out. Oh..."

Mary was rambling in an effort to describe the man, explaining as if everything would be all right if only she could make this person known to Bill.

Silently, I prayed that it would be alright, but in my heart I knew it was already too late for Lexy. I wanted to do something. I wanted to help these frantic people.

"What's his name? Does anyone here know his name, where he's staying?" Bill inquired of Mary and the large crowd of students that had gathered 'round.

There was a murmur amongst the students. Finally, someone came forward.

"Terry Brown's his name. I think he's staying at 'The Pink Flamingo' around the corner. Stays there, I think," the slightly flustered student supplied.

50

"Oh God," Bill sighed. "Evie, Hilly, Mary—would you mind calling him? Getting him over here. I've got to talk with him immediately."

"I'll call," I volunteered. I didn't feel much like part of the group now. "You stay and help reassure the kids; I'll try and locate the fellow." I went to the main desk in the lobby for the number of the hotel.

I tapped my foot impatiently as I let the phone ring off the hook. Finally, the manager came back on the line and in a very annoyed, strained voice told me there was no answer in that room.

I told him it was an emergency, pressed him for information. Finally, reluctantly, he told me that Terry Brown had been there earlier, entertaining a girlfriend, rather intoxicated but still able to function. He told me he could put me through to Terry's friend who might know more.

"He's in room, ah, 136, ma'am. I'll put the call through for you, miss."

This time the phone was snapped up on the first ring.

"Hello, hello, Terry?"

Startled at the instant response and desperation in the man's voice, I couldn't think what to say at first.

Stalling a moment while I gathered my wits, I introduced myself. Then quickly explained the situation as best I could.

He didn't say anything while I spoke; then I heard, "On my way...."

The line went dead as I held the phone in my hand. Very slowly, I replaced the receiver back on its cradle. From the way Terry's friend had answered the call it was clear that he too was awake and worried about his friend's whereabouts.

51

CHAPTER NINE

Bill sent the students back upstairs to their rooms. He also sent me to my room, telling me there was nothing I could do now. He'd call me if things changed.

Upset and worried sick for Lexy, I couldn't sleep, I didn't change out of my clothes for fear that I would be called on and have to take valuable time to dress. I lay fully clothed on top of my bed.

Though it was a warm night, I was cold and lay shivering on top of the covers. Once, I got up and went to the sliding glass door that led to the front balcony. I looked to the ocean and the moon's reflection on the peaceful water. I looked up to the sky and prayed. Then I pulled the drapes and returned to my bed. This time, I slipped my sandals off and got under the covers.

I don't know how long I lay there, eyes wide open though I was exhausted to the bone. Somewhere in the very early morning hours, I fell asleep. Suddenly, I awoke with a jolt.

I looked around my room. Strong sunlight beat at the corners of the curtains and drapes, begging to be let in.

"What time is it?" I asked myself and glanced at my watch.

"Oh my God!" I exclaimed as I saw it was after 9 a.m.

What was going on? Why hadn't anyone awakened me? Surely, they had to know something by now. "Surely they found Lexy—found her safe and sound." I mumbled to myself as I leapt out of bed and flew around the room. Briefly, when I got a look at myself in the mirror, I thought of changing out of my wrinkled clothes.

"Waste of time," I muttered as I shook my head, hoping that my hair didn't always look this bad in the morning.

"Stop it, stop it," I chastised myself. I knew that I cared nothing about my hair. I was just trying to think of something other than what was really on my mind—scaring the liver out of me.

Without thinking, I grabbed my bag and headed out the door. I didn't know where I was going, but I needed to find Bill, Hilly, Mary—someone who could tell me what they'd found out.

I went to their rooms first. No answer at Bill's, no answer at Mary and Hilly's. I didn't dare ask any of the students.

I flew down the stairs, not wanting to wait for the elevator.

When I got to the lobby, I gasped. There was absolute pandemonium. I could see chaperones and adults herding and whispering and everyone pushing to the lobby desk. The harried clerk was nodding and trying to accommodate people, while the phone behind the desk rang off the hook.

Desperately I looked around for someone I could talk to. I needed to find out what had happened but there was no one that didn't have his hands full, literally and figuratively. Now I was almost frantic. I couldn't imagine what was going on.

Where is Bill? my mind screamed. *Not identifying Lexy's body,* I prayed. *Oh God, please, no.*

I found that I was near panic. I had to get a hold of myself or I'd just add to the problems here. With great effort I tried to calm myself down.

When I thought I was in control I made my way around the large room, stopping from time-to-time trying to eavesdrop on the emotional, jumbled conversations that were taking place. All the while, I kept my eyes peeled for Bill. Mary and Hilly were in the midst of the crowd. There was no way I could get to them and ask them any questions.

Suddenly there was a murmur and I turned in the direction that all the heads turned—toward a small conference room that led off the lobby.

A man and a woman, both in sunglasses, emerged with a small figure between them. Head bent, horribly pale, shaking visibly, Lexy took tiny steps as she slowly walked with her escorts. Behind them came a very somber Bill.

The lobby was quiet now except for an occasional nervous cough.

My God, please, someone tell me what's happened! My mind screamed in frustration for the umpteenth time.

I slumped into a lobby chair and waited, contented for the moment that Lexy was not dead. I had to be patient. Someone would eventually get to me. In the meantime it was enough to know that my worst fears had been unfounded.

Whatever happened, she is alive and will heal, I thought to myself.

I watched as if I was in a dream state. Everything in front of me looked like it unfolded in slow motion. People whispered to one another, gently pushing their charges this way and that. Some of the students' faces were pinched and angry, some devoid of expression. There was an unintelligible buzz of voices in the background. I thought I might be at an Alfred Hitchcock movie or maybe at the outer limits of the twilight zone....

Somehow, all my strength was gone. I sat alone and mute until the lobby was empty and I was aware that I was back in real time. My senses had returned to normal, or so it seemed.

In all that time, though I didn't know how much time had passed since I'd raced to the lobby to find this crazy scene, no one had approached me, no one had spoken to me. It was as if I did not exist for these people.

Is everyone in shock? I found myself wondering. I saw Bill, Mary and Hilly walk through the door from outside. They seemed a little calmer now that the masses had dispersed. All were obviously shaken, but seemed to have themselves and their feelings in check.

After all, I reminded myself, *they are professionals and experienced chaperones.*

Suddenly I found myself not wanting to make the first move, not wanting to know what had occurred to bring about this unbelievable scene. I wished I was invisible now. I tried to push my chair closer to the wall; it was as close as it could get. I cleared my throat nervously, and with head bowed, I stared at my hands in my lap. Somehow I had managed to bite all my nails to nubs—I hadn't even realized it until now.

I shifted in my seat. I felt like an intruder. I didn't want my friends to have to deal with me after all they'd obviously been through. I felt guilty for my presence in this difficult time.

I was in the way, big, obtuse, selfish... my mind chided. All the while in the background, *You don't want to know, you don't want to know...Lexy's alive—you saw her. It is enough!*

I closed my eyes. I could sense the three chaperones standing around me. *Go away. Just go away*, a voice inside my head screamed.

"Evie, come along." It was Bill's voice. Still I sat in my chair, eyes closed, praying that they would go on and leave me be...protect me from hearing what I didn't want to hear. Everything was fine now because Lexy was alive. It's all I needed to know.

"Evie, come upstairs with us. We'll talk—tell you what's happened. Just not here. "

I felt soft hands slip into mine. I chanced a look—Mary on one side, Hilly on the other. I said nothing, just followed obediently as I was led. No one spoke as we got into the empty elevator. Someone pushed a button. I kept my eyes trained on the tiles on the floor. I felt as though Bounder had just died and I was alone...alone and traumatized, my life meaningless and pathetic.

The recent events had taken a toll on me, conspired against me. In an effort to put my past behind me, I'd forgotten it—thought it was safely put away. My mind knew otherwise. It would not let me forget so easily.

The elevator stopped; the door opened. The four of us stepped out.

I took a deep, ragged breath and pushed my shoulders back. I would not allow the poor soul from Ohio back into my life.

We walked two-by-two down the corridor. Hilly was beside me now. Every once in awhile I could see her cast a sideways glance in my direction. While we waited at the door for Mary to unlock their room, I smiled reassuringly.

Once inside, everyone except Bill sat down. I found a chair by the closet and Hilly and Mary each sat on a bed.

Bill cleared his throat.

"Evie, I wanted to take you aside and let you know what had happened to Lexy. I will be taking what's left of our group and leaving the island. Our plane leaves at noon. As you saw earlier, many of the students have gone already.

"We had a parents' retreat on Eleuthra, one of the outer islands, that coincided with the kids' break...we got in touch with them and they flew in... chartered a plane...."

He was rambling, unfocused. Hilly started to say something to him, "Bill, get to..."

Bill looked at her, surprised to see her sitting on the bed. "Oh, sorry," he apologized, "a little tired...."

He straightened and seemed to be gathering his thoughts; then he went on.

"Lexy and Terry somehow ended up on the beach last night. It appears as though they took a moonlit walk and in their drunken stupor, they lay down on the beach to rest or neck or whatever. Lexy had forgotten, or wasn't capable of realizing, the danger she was in. Or maybe she felt safe with Terry. It doesn't really matter now."

Bill cleared his throat then continued.

"Anyway, they both passed out apparently. And sometime early in the morning, after the casinos on Paradise Island closed, Lexy was found half-naked, confused, wandering in the middle of Sand Street.

"Two croupiers from the casino saw her and stopped. They picked her up and put her in their car and took her to one of the dancer's apartments in downtown Nassau. Apparently, the dancer was able to determine that Lexy had been carried from the beach to a vacant beach house across the street. There, she was raped repeatedly by a gang, maybe six or seven young Bahamians. She...."

I gasped, and then put my hand to my lips to prevent anymore unexpected outbursts. I shuddered as I thought about poor Lexy enduring this horrible experience. Tears welled in my eyes. I was careful to breathe slowly and not blink. I did not want the tears to roll down my face.

Bill looked at me to see if I was okay and I nodded my head for him to continue. "Don't ask me why but the dancer took it upon herself to clean Lexy up and to bathe her. The toiletry included a good strong douche."

I was shocked and couldn't help but look at my two female companions for their reaction. They both shook their heads, just as incredulous at this chain of events as I was. No one spoke for some time; then Bill went on.

"One of the croupiers called me and told me that he had a member of my group. He said he'd bring her to the hotel and we could talk. He also said he had a friend who was a reporter and he wanted to give Lexy's story to this person to publish."

"Why on earth…," I stammered.

"This political mess, I guess. They wanted the bad publicity to undo some of the momentum that the Black party has gathered. So close to the election, they thought Lexy's story might sway some of the voters to vote white and stir up all kinds of animosity between the parties' followers."

"I told the guy we'd discuss it, and, of course, Lexy would have to give permission. I knew we'd have nothing to do with this, but I didn't want the guy to keep Lexy or get the reporter to her before I had her back and we could determine what was best for her.

"She was returned by the dancer. The croupiers apparently didn't want to be seen. When I saw Lexy, it was clear she was in shock. But when she said, 'Terry,' I knew that we didn't know what happened to him. I asked the dancer if she'd seen a man wandering around.

"All hell let loose when we sent a party down to the beach and Terry was there broken and bloody. He'd been savagely attacked—by whom we don't know. The island gendarmes are looking into it. They doubt it was the same bunch that attacked Lexy, but they won't be sure until they find those that took her to the beach house."

Bill shook his head. "Terry's in the local hospital now and will be for a while, but he should recover from his injuries in time.

"Lexy's parents flew in from Eleuthra and they wanted to get their daughter away from this frightening place as soon as possible. They left just after the police allowed them to go."

"My God," I whispered under my breath. I was speechless. I simply didn't know what to say about such awful, incredible events. And, poor Alexis, poor, poor Lexy...."

CHAPTER TEN

I was listless and depressed for days after my friends left. I wandered around my room and out onto the balcony thinking of Lexy and the terrible ordeal she'd suffered. I prayed that what had occurred would not dampen her inherently trusting and playful nature. I couldn't bear the thought that she might not recover emotionally from the trauma of the invasive incidents—that she might lose her fun-loving outlook on life. I'd learned so much from her and I felt that I owed her my own progress, in part, because we'd come together briefly and she'd allowed me to share her spirit.

I found that I could not help putting myself in her place. I went over and over what happened to her that night—at least what I knew of it—and I was devastated for her. I hoped that Alexis was a better and braver person. I thought about her escort that fateful evening—how was he faring? And would Lexy blame herself for his misfortune? I prayed for them.

I ate some, but not much. I no longer enjoyed myself. With the departure of my friends and under the circumstances they left, there was a great sadness surrounding me. Finally, I withdrew from the balcony, drew my drapes and kept my room darkened against the sea. Although, there was life still going on around me, I chose not to be included. I slept or rested a lot and often pulled out my brooch to stare at it mutely. I didn't comprehend its significance in my present state of mind.

It is a thing; human life was ever so much more valuable, I thought as I stood fingering the object and thinking again about Lexy and all those people that her violation had hurt.

I really didn't understand the political situation and I thoroughly failed to see why it would help the natives' party to hurt the tourist trade. It made no sense. I did not like aggression, violence, intimidation, prejudice. It seemed to me life was indeed tough enough without adding all these negative elements. Of course, the black leaders had denounced the intimidation and repeated harassments directed at the white visitors, but all continued and therefore, I concluded, they must have secretly approved the tactics.

I stood in front of the mirror on the bureau. I saw the Ohio Old Maid, as I'd come to call myself before I'd experienced the wonders of the New York makeover's magic. Once again, I thought back to the days immediately after my parents' death, then to Bounder. I smiled sadly at the memories. I thought about the dangling wire and I was brought up short.

What had happened to my resolution to live... to experience life with risk and adversity... to feel and participate in the ultimate game? I shook my head, clucking at that old woman with the chicken wire hairs in her head.

While I stood there, many thoughts came to my mind— most unbidden. But I let them flow through as I strengthened my resolve. I didn't know if I would see my new friends again. Their leaving had been hurried but they'd taken time to plan a visit in the summer—to Hilly's house in Maine. These three were co-workers, but over the years they'd taught, worked and traveled together, they'd forged a strong bond of friendship.

Some years ago they started having annual summer outings at Hilly's island cottage. I was touched they'd invited me but doubted I'd join them. I had Hilly's address on Sterling's Island and phone number and the dates that Mary and Bill were planning to visit her. I didn't know if I really wanted to be reminded of this whole thing again, and I didn't think I'd like Maine.

"Isn't it on the end of the earth, anyway?" I asked the pale, unsmiling face in the mirror. "What in the world would I find to do in Maine?"

"Well," I mused, "it's nice to have the opportunity to see Hilly, Mary and Bill again if I want." I decided that it was a fine gesture that they'd given me a connection to them in spite of everything they'd just been through and in all the commotion of leave-taking. They were good people.

"Yes, very nice," I said aloud to the empty room.

I gave a last, furtive look at the figure in the mirror and turned away. I pulled my bags from under the bed and began to pull things from them. Sometime in the last couple of days I'd packed—especially all my brightly-colored clothing. I hadn't wanted it around to remind me that this tropical paradise was not all that it seemed.

I selected an outfit and hung it on the back of the bathroom door. I took a long, lukewarm shower and hoped that maybe some of the wrinkles would come out of my sundress. As I stepped from the shower I thought of Lexy again; somehow I felt that she would be okay. She was that type of woman. I guess I realized that she was no longer a girl, that her ordeal had elevated her status. But I felt that she would not only survive it, somehow she would be stronger. She would be fine, and, I believed, so would Terry.

I smiled as I dried off. I knew that Alexis would be okay and so would I. I was determined to think positive.

I dressed and primped before the mirror. I opened my drapes as I planned to open myself to experience what was out there. I took the Do Not Disturb sign on my door and flipped it over so that the maid would be notified to clean the room. For an instant, I wondered if they'd been bothered by that sign's presence for several days. Had they been glad that there was that much less work for them to do—or had they wondered about the occupant within?

Quickly, I locked the door and skipped down the corridor.

"Life is what you make it!" I said to no one in particular. I worked on my attitude all the way to the lobby.

I stopped feeling alone and sorry for myself the minute I stepped from the hotel onto the sidewalk. The sun was magnificent, warm and nurturing. There was a whisper of a breeze which combined with the gentle, sweet smell of local flowers from nearby gardens. The total effect was heavenly. I looked to the sky and saw the clear blue of a perfect horizon.

I turned the corner and headed to Lums for a Lumdog with extra sauerkraut, even though I wasn't all that fond of it. I just felt capricious and like overdoing it. "Why not?" I smiled, proud of my progress so far.

And, I'd have a whole pitcher of beer to myself, I thought as I wandered along oblivious to my surroundings. I knew the route to Lums by heart and I just let my feet take me there while my mind made me promises. I put all unpleasant thoughts from my mind and concentrated on enjoying myself.

Suddenly, I felt a sharp pain in my groin and I gasped. I looked up to see a native boy. He couldn't have been more than twelve or thirteen—although they always seemed to look younger than they really were.

"Hey," I yelled at him, shocked at his action and angry because he not only hurt me but was perpetrating this ongoing hostility.

"Why'd you do that to me?" I shouted, not expecting to get an answer and having no idea why I'd just tried to communicate with someone who'd attacked me.

He stuck his face right into mine. His eyes were maybe an inch from my own. He leered at me—a nasty, grown-up leer filled with hatred.

His look took me aback but I didn't move. I don't know what I was thinking at that exact moment or why I did what I did next. And I was totally unaware of the small crowd of tourists that was quickly gathering around this scene. The only thing that existed at this moment were the two of us— head-to-head in a posture of aggression.

I reached out and grabbed his groin, and, like the dangling wire in my Ohio attic, I gave it a squeeze with all my might.

His eyes grew large with surprise, then registered pain and finally, he howled like a wounded animal.

"I wondered how you'd like it...." I said innocently.

He was heading in the opposite direction now, limping as fast as he could with his hands between his legs. And once or twice he looked back over his shoulder at me. I thought his eyes still registered shock and surprise. Oddly enough, the hatred of only a moment before was gone.

The people around me were clapping and I became aware of them for the first time. I smiled timidly and hurried to get to Lum's. I barely heard the words that the crowd shouted after me.

"Well done!" and "Bravo!" and even a "Way to go, lady," from a young surfer type.

I was suddenly ashamed of myself. Why had I done such a thing? After all, I was a grown woman and this was just a boy. I had no right to put a hand on him or hurt him the way I did. I was still thinking about the unexpected way I'd acted when I walked into Lums and was immediately seated. I knew the menu by heart and ordered without looking at it. As I waited for my food to be served, I continued to think about what had just transpired.

Jesus, why should I feel guilty? I asked myself while I waited to be served. *I didn't initiate it and I didn't ask for it. And, besides, he did something to me that a boy shouldn't have done. It was right,* I guessed, *that I'd treated him as he treated me....*

My order came and I quickly poured the chilled beer from the pitcher to the frosted mug. I lifted the mug and took a long pull on the salty liquid. *It was the best tasting brew in the world,* I thought happily.

Absentmindedly, I used my fingers to wipe away most of the extra, sauerkraut I'd ordered on my Lumdog. I put my fingers to my mouth and began to lick off the bits of sauerkraut that stuck to my fingers. Soon, I was trying to get the stuff off my cheek.

How do I make such messes? I asked myself happily.

"Excuse me. Is this seat taken?"

I knew immediately who that voice belonged to.

Shit! I hadn't seen him come in. Hadn't thought much about him since I'd seen him at the Drum Beat Club and Bill had pulled me away. I'd lost all recollection of him when this Lexy business started. And now, here he was standing in front of me waiting for me to invite him to join me. And here I was with a half-full pitcher of beer in front of me and my fingers in my mouth.

Oh, I groaned inwardly. *Why me? Why do these things have to happen to me?* I removed my fingers from my mouth and brushed at the side of my cheek where I thought a piece of sauerkraut rested; then I attempted a casual smile.

"Well, sure," I said and gestured with my other hand to the seat across from me. He pulled out the chair beside me and sat down.

Under the table, I felt for the napkin. I had to get that stuff off my fingers. What if he tried to hold my hand or something? I gave up on trying to find the napkin. I used my sun dress instead.

"Care for some beer?" I offered.

"Why don't I order my own pitcher," he smiled. "I will be sure to get some that way. ..."

Oh my God, I thought again.

This man was incredible. He had such an easy, charming manner and he simply made me melt. I found myself wishing I could get away from him, but I knew I wouldn't have changed places at this moment with anyone else—not for all the world.

Was this the adventure I'd waited for all my long, dull life? Would this man even want to be my friend, let alone my lover?

My mind was racing and I flushed with embarrassment as I realized the heat my thoughts generated.

"Sauerkraut?" I asked and pointed to mound of it beside my still untouched Lumdog. I knew I could not eat the Lumdog now. This man's presence made me a basket case. I had all I could do to manage the mug—a Lumdog was out of the question.

He laughed a big, hearty laugh and touched me on the shoulder.

"You're something, you are," he smiled affectionately.

I giggled.

This was ludicrous. This man was smooth and polished and here I was this bumbling middle-aged idiot from the Midwest—out for the first and last big adventure of my life. *Why doesn't he just go away and let me get on with it?* my mind screamed.

"Two more," I heard him say.

"Lumdogs, mister?" came the waiter's reply.

He laughed. "No, pitchers," he said and gave my arm a gentle squeeze.

"We might as well enjoy ourselves, don't you think?" he asked softly.

I couldn't speak. This fellow was so disarmingly charming. Without apparent effort, he seemed to know just what to say.

"I haven't had a beer breakfast in some time," he said, matter-of-factly. "Actually, come to think of it, this is my first ever."

His first ever! God, I loved the way he said that.

I sat quietly and guzzled my beer.

Soon I realized I had to go to the bathroom.

"Excuse me," I said as I got up and headed for the ladies' room. I heard him say something but didn't want to ask him to repeat it so I hurried on. I knew I was in trouble here—that man had such an effect on me, I could barely function.

67

When I was safely inside the powder room, I leaned against the cool wall to catch my breath. Then I picked the nearest stall and hovered above the toilet seat.

"Well, doesn't that beat all!" I said in frustration as I squatted awkwardly above the bowl.

"Pardon me!" came a mature, cultured voice from the adjoining stall.

"Oh, nothing." I said. "Just talking to myself."

I couldn't believe that I wasn't able to pee. My body was conspiring against me. *All that beer*, I wondered, *where had it gone?*

Finally, I couldn't hover any longer. My legs were beginning to tremble with the effort of keeping my body suspended over that darned toilet bowl. I straightened up and flushed the toilet, then left the stall.

Without looking up, I stood at the wash basin and finally got the sauerkraut juice off my fingers. When I was finished washing my hands, I glanced at the mirror and then turned round quickly to see if that was someone else's neck I saw there. No one stood behind me so I slowly returned my gaze back to my own reflection.

What I saw was not to be believed. I had never seen anything like it. My neck was covered with these large red blotches!

I was distracted momentarily by the flushing of the toilet in the still-occupied stall. I looked into the mirror to see a tall, lovely older lady emerging.

Gracefully, she walked over to the basin next to mine. I studied her in the mirror. She was so lovely with her beautiful silver hair and brilliant hazel eyes. Her tanned face made her all the more elegant. She smiled with an all-knowing expression on her face.

"Nerves?" she asked gesturing toward my neck.

"What?" I asked, aghast.

I returned my eyes to the ugly red blotches all over my neck. I wasn't sure if it was my imagination, but they looked a little redder with all the attention—and they were beginning to itch. I reached my hand to scratch them.

"No, no, that will just make them worse, my dear. Ignore them. They'll just go away...in time," she added.

I looked at her blankly.

"I've never had anything like this before."

"Hives, I think," she responded as she pulled a compact out of her straw purse and casually began to touch-up her flawless complexion.

"Hives?" I asked, stunned.

"Yes, my dear—that's what I think. I used to get them myself when I was younger."

"Really? Why?"

"Well, I got them every time I was around this certain man," she supplied graciously.

"What did you do?" I asked incredulous at the information she shared with me.

"Well, I married him, of course," she said as she tucked her compact back in her purse and winked at me. Half a second later I was alone.

"Hives," I said flatly. "That's all I need now."

Then it struck me. It was stupid to concern myself with this. That guy was not going to stick around for this country bumpkin. Surely he'd had time to think things through while I was otherwise occupied. He'd be gone by the time I got back.

He was still there, calmly sipping from his frosty mug. He'd done a fair job of draining his pitcher, too.

He smiled and stood when he saw me.

"I was beginning to wonder if you were ever coming back," he said as he pulled my chair out.

When I didn't reply, he said, "I've been thinking...."

"Ummmm," I responded noncommittally.

"Well, some friends and I are going to do some sailing and I was wondering if you'd like to join us.

"Actually," he continued without waiting for me to answer, "they've flown to Tortola to pick up a 48' Bristol near the bareboat charter business over there. They should be here by this afternoon. Then we'll be leaving Nassau and cruising the islands and beautiful Caribbean waters for the next week or so. What do you say, will you join us?"

I stared at him. Obviously he was out of his mind.

"I couldn't possibly join you and your friends on a boat for a week," I said.

"Why on earth not?" he asked seriously. "Do you have other plans? A better offer?" He looked hurt.

"Well, I don't even know your name!" I nearly shouted at him.

"It's ah, Slade. Ah, Slade Williams."

I looked at him nonplussed.

Of course his name would be Slade Williams—like something right out of a Harlequin Romance novel. Honestly, he looked the part and his name and demeanor were right. I didn't have a chance.

I swallowed hard as I prepared my next objection.

"These friends of yours—how long have you known them?" And then it dawned on me that they were probably all men and of course I couldn't possibly spend a week or so on a boat with all these men—especially when I didn't know them.

"Actually not that long. I really just met them briefly a couple years ago. Then I met them again last week before they left to pick up the boat. We discovered we have the same alma mater, but they were there several years after I graduated." He cleared his throat a little self-consciously. "This time I met them in a *bar* on Paradise Island of all places!" He emphasized *bar* and winked at me.

I couldn't speak—just sat there looking at him and felt my color deepen in reaction to him.

Fortunately, he seemed not to notice his effect on me and kept talking.

"There are two girls and a guy—seem like nice people. But one of the girls may not be going, and if so it would just be the four of us. I think you'd have a great time. Will you go?"

"Why not?" I heard a voice saying and I could not believe the voice had come from my mouth.

CHAPTER ELEVEN

"What is wrong with you?" I asked myself in the mirror.

I had bolted down the end of my pitcher of beer and left Lums with my new-found escort. He was right now waiting downstairs in the lobby of my hotel. I was supposed to pack and check out and we were on our way. He, apparently, was all ready to go.

I brought myself closer to the mirror and studied my face and neck. Unbelievably, the rosy blotches were still there—less obvious, yes, but still quite noticeable.

"Aren't I awfully unwise to be taking a cruise with a man who is capable of doing this to me without so much as the slightest physical contact? And," I continued to talk with myself, "what on earth will happen if he should actually touch me?"

I'll probably throw up, I thought glumly as I turned from the mirror and took a last look around the room.

I looked down at my blue-and-white rope sandals, straightened my navy-blue shorts and smoothed the collar on my white midi-blouse. I was in my most nautical outfit and I was ready. With much bravado I did not feel, I picked up my bags and headed to the lobby to meet my fate.

All the way down, I kept thinking, "How bad can this be? It's the chance of a lifetime—a potentially excellent adventure—the things memories are made of...."

I reassured myself that with two other women and one other man, I would be quartered with the women. I knew nothing about boats, especially how they were set up. I'd only spent time on short sails on the Charles back east, and if I knew anything, I'd surely forgotten it. Oh.

Whatever the sleeping accommodations are—I reasoned, *I would be able to have my own bed or bunk or whatever it is they call it on a ship.*

When I reached the lobby and saw Slade standing there waiting patiently, I nearly turned and ran back to my room. There was no way I could avoid making a fool of myself with this man and I desperately did not want to do that!

What in God's name was I going to do with myself while I was in close quarters with a man who could make my heart skip a beat just by smiling? What on earth was I going to do?

I started to turn around—to beat a hasty retreat before he spotted me. I just didn't have the nerve to go off with this incredible stranger or the desire to shame myself in front of him and his friends. I simply could not go through with this. *It was ludicrous, what was I thinking when I agreed to this?*

Then I remembered the pitcher-and-a-half of beer I'd inhaled and that sort of explained things to me. I'd been drunk, plain and simple. I pushed the button, for the elevator. I would return to my room, call down to the desk and have the man there make my apologies for me.

"Oh there you are! I was beginning to think maybe you were having second thoughts about this and were going to chicken out and leave me, ah, wanting—waiting," he quickly corrected himself.

"Not me!" I laughed nervously. I was doomed, but I had to admit, it was a hell of a way to go—death by physical intoxication from the opposite sex. I wondered if anything like that had ever occurred? If not, I was sure to be the first. The Gingerman walked toward me, took me by the arm and steered me to the checkout desk. He appeared not to be taking any chances from this point on. It was as if he could read my mind.

Now that's really all I need, I thought as I withdrew my traveler's checks from my bag.

"All taken care of, ma'am," the desk clerk smiled at me, even as he winked conspiratorially at Slade. I was shocked.

"What? I... I...." and I was still stammering when the man behind the counter explained that the gentleman on my arm had paid the bill.

"Slade?" I thought and wondered why in heaven's name he'd want to do that.

"We're in a hurry, young lady," he said to me as he spirited me through the lobby, out the door and into a waiting taxi.

"Well, thank you. I'll reimburse you as soon as we get settled," I said feeling somewhat guilty. I didn't know whether it was from his paying my bill or because I thought I was making him late for the rendezvous with his friends or....

We rode in silence the rest of the way to the pier. When the cab stopped, I glanced at the meter and stuffed some bills into the cabbie's hand.

"There!" I said, and stepped from the cab onto the old, sturdy wooden wharf. The Gingerman followed behind me shaking his head.

"You really are something," he said softly. I thought I detected admiration in his voice.

I had intended to march down the pier and brightly smile and wave to his companions as I lightly jumped aboard the boat. But as I looked down the pier there were at least half a dozen boats of various shapes, sizes and colors lining each side of the pier.

I hadn't wanted Slade to know just how much out of my element I was. I wanted him to think I was fun and game and could handle anything comfortably. I knew he'd find out the truth sooner or later. I was just hoping it would be later.

"Oh well," I sighed to myself and turned to him for directions.

"Straight ahead, down the ramp on the left and it's the long, blue boat on the end. The one with those two idiots hoisting a cocktail flag on the stern," he smiled at me.

I was still staring at him. There he was lugging all my baggage as well as a couple of his own. I'd totally forgotten about my luggage.

"Oh, oh, here, let me take something," I offered.

"I'm all set," he smiled winningly.

I turned and marched toward my objective. At the top of the pier by the ramp I rested my arm casually against an old piling. I stood gazing at the beautiful sights around me while I waited for Slade to catch up.

When he was a step or two behind me I made the half-turn onto the ramp.

"Ouch!" I gasped as a small wooden splinter from the piling tore into my wrist and a trickle of blood slid down my arm.

"You okay?"

"Ah, yah," I said as I glanced at my wrist. "I got a little

cut here, that's all. It's nothing." I pulled a Kleenex out of my pocket, pressed it to the cut, and continued on down the ramp to the float.

"Don't worry. We'll clean it up when we're aboard. I've got just the thing..." his voice trailed off.

I was in front of a huge boat. The two people standing there with hands out looked like ants on this monster of a boat.

"Hi! I'm Slade's, ah, friend, Evie Moore."

"Welcome aboard. I'm Patty or Paddy. I'll answer to either," said the young man, smiling. His extended hand grabbed mine and he fairly swept me through a small opening in the wire railing.

I was aboard.

Suddenly I was face-to-face with the girl beside him. She was striking in an unusual way. She was young, maybe late twenties, with cat-green eyes in an impossibly freckled face. Her hair was Shirley Temple style with bright red ringlets— she looked like a living doll at about five feet tall. My first reaction was to hug her; I wondered how she affected men. She was just so cute that I couldn't help my response to her even though I was embarrassed and surprised by it.

"Cat, short for Catherine," she introduced herself with a grin and squeezed my arm. "You're just...well, adorable," I couldn't help saying to her. I blushed in embarrassment at my words.

"Oh, everyone says that when they meet Bish," replied Patty. "But it soon changes," he laughed, "once they get to know her, that is!" he added playfully, the dimples in his cheeks showing.

Everyone laughed.

Bish? I thought, and as if Cat had read my mind, she

quickly supplied the answer. "Short for Bishop. We're very fond of our nicknames where I come from," Cat said proudly.

"Ah, I see introductions have been made. Patty, shall we get underway so as not to delay cocktail hour?" Slade asked. I was so mesmerized by Cat's unique looks that I hadn't even noticed Slade get on the boat.

"Sure," Patty said agreeably, and added, "Cat will show you around, Evie. Slade and I will motor out of here. We'll set the sails once we get out of the inner harbor—away from the congestion. It's easier that way," he explained, then caught sight of the Kleenex clinging to my wrist.

"Hey, what did you do to your arm? Hell, we haven't even left the dock and you're already hurt!"

I'd forgotten about my scrape. Quickly, I removed the Kleenex, which was sticking to the small cut, and saw that I was no longer bleeding. I showed everyone so they'd see I was fine indeed. I smiled and put the blood-spotted Kleenex into my pocket. I didn't know what else to do with it. I glanced around nervously. I wasn't comfortable with all the attention.

Cat and Paddy smiled at me; Slade was shaking his head and grinning.

She and I picked up the bags Slade had left on the deck while he got ready to untie the lines and cast off.

Cat led me down some steep steps and into the main salon. I stared in amazement at the large comfortable chairs, the L-shaped dinette, the glistening mahogany.

"I can't believe this!"

"Cozy, huh?" Cat asked as she pointed out the various creature comforts. "And roomy. We can open this table up to seat six if we want. Not only that but it can be turned into a double bed! We can sleep seven people in here."

"I don't know anything about boats," I admitted but that didn't seem to faze her.

"Slade didn't think you did," she responded casually. "But that doesn't matter. By the time we're through, you'll be an old salt!" she exclaimed with an all-knowing smile. "In another life, Patty and I used to sell these things—beautiful boats...," she said with a bit of wistfulness in her voice.

I let the comment about Slade pass—it made no sense. "Now, step into my galley. Oh," she interrupted herself. "I forgot to mention the coffee maker and microwave in the salon. And, now to one of my favorite parts of the boat— the galley. Look at this, gas stove with three burners, oven, broiler, double sinks here, oh and propane grill hanging off the stern rail...."

"Wow!" was all I could manage. She was so enthusiastic as she pointed here and there that I couldn't follow all the things she was saying and pointing out. But I was so overwhelmed, I decided it really didn't matter.

"Head over here, we've got two," she said as she continued down a long, long passageway. I looked around— it was just awesome, like an enclosed alley. "Excuse me, head?" I queried.

"Yes, W.C., lav, bathroom...."

"Oh, I see," and I did when she turned a small handle on the wall and the door fell open to reveal a shower, sink and toilet.

"Here, give me your arm," she said. She'd already grabbed a bottle of alcohol and a tissue and begun dabbing it on my wrist.

"Oh, that's nothing,"

"Well, it's all too easy to get an infection—no sense taking any chances. There!" she exclaimed as she completed her task and put the alcohol back under the lavatory sink. "Now you know where it is if you need it again."

She ushered me out of the head and closed the door.

"How long is this, ah, vessel?" I asked as we continued down the long corridor.

"Forty-seven feet and seven inches exactly. It's a Bristol 48—that's the make, Bristol. And the 48 is the length. We always round the inches up to make even feet," she spoke easily, completely at home in these surroundings.

I couldn't help thinking she must have been one hell of a salesperson.

We continued on.

"We stowed our gear in the stern—the aft cabin; it's behind the stateroom. We'll give you a tour later.

"You guys get the v-berth," she said and opened another door to reveal the most inviting room. It was huge and I could even see a TV and VCR up on the shelf.

"Wow," I said again, in awe. It was as beautiful and homey as any room I'd ever seen.

"Yes," she said, "I think you'll be real comfortable here. And, look here." She reached up and unlatched something, then gave a push and there was a skylight.

"A hatch for star-gazing," she laughed.

"Oh," I was confused. It was like she was speaking another language. I didn't understand half the terms she used, and I didn't know what to think about the 'berth' arrangements. But I did like the idea of having one bed against one wall of the boat and the other on the opposite side—a perfect 'V'.

"What happened to the other girl?" I wondered aloud. "I was sure the CC and Gingerman said there'd be two other girls with him and his friend."

"The what? CC and...."

"Gingerman," I supplied, unaware until now that I'd let that slip.

"Slade," I said apologetically.

"Oh, that's wonderful," she enthused. "Do tell me all about this nickname of yours. I told you how much we like our nicknames."

"I love it!" She added after I'd quickly filled her in on how Slade had bought me my first drink in the New York airport lounge. "It's really wonderful. Slade is so...so... oh, I don't know, like a character out of a Harlequin Romance novel or something," she continued.

I knew right then and there that she and I would be good friends. She had a delicious sense of humor which I appreciated and we seemed to think alike.

"Well, now," she continued right back on track. "Now what shall we call him? *CC!*" she cried out.

"Or the Gingerman?" I asked, finishing her thought.

"Or maybe just plain Ginger," she giggled.

At that we both laughed uproariously.

"Hey, what's going on down there?"

We turned in unison and could see Slade bending down above the steps leading to the salon. He looked like he was a mile away.

At the sight of him, we laughed harder. But we did start making our way toward him.

"Hey, you two aren't keeping up your end of the bargain! We're under way, it's cocktail hour, and you two wenches are down here making merry. The crew is THIRSTY!" he roared, in mock irritation.

I'd been barely aware that the motor had stopped. Then, there had been a lot of clanging and lurching and the pull of wind in sail as the boat caught its own natural rhythm and began riding the sea. Suddenly it dawned on me that the engines were no longer running—we were sailing. I couldn't wait to get on deck and look and feel the sensation for the first time. I'd been so intent on my first look around a boat that I'd barely noticed the changes occurring around me.

"Oh," I exclaimed in glee. "I can't wait to get upstairs and look around. This is wonderful and...exciting!"

"Certainly is—a whole new way of life, my dear. I think you'll be enjoying this sailing stuff, especially when we get topside," Cat teased.

"I know I have a lot to learn," I admitted, "but at least I know one thing—I like this feeling."

"Well, you'll like it even better when I get these drinks made and we can relax and properly enjoy the act of. What will you have?"

"Gee, I don't know. What do you recommend?"

"How 'bout a CC and Ginger-man?" she asked with a huge smile.

"Perfect," I replied without missing a beat.

"Okay, I'll be bartender, you waitress. That way I can get to Patty sooner and tell him this Gingerman story and we can decide on a nickname for Slade."

Inwardly I groaned—she really was serious about sharing this story and giving Slade an honest-to-goodness nickname. I was too embarrassed to ask her not do that. It was my own damn fault anyway.

While she mixed the drinks, I changed the subject.

"How did you meet Paddy anyway? Where is the other girl that Slade said was sailing with us?"

Before she could answer, Slade was back in the galley hatch and doing his best to scowl.

"Ladies, ladies, P-L-E-A-S-E, me mate and I are hankerin' for some of that thar dark rum." He spoke like Long John Silver and even rolled out the 'r' in rum as he pointed to the bottle Cat was pouring into the ice-laden glasses.

I bowed and scraped as I imagined a galley slave would and then Slade was gone. Cat and I looked at one another and broke into peals of laughter again.

"Here, all set, let's take these damn things up before they decide to keel haul us. You take this one—it's for Slade. I guess we'll have to finish our conversation later, when Captain Bly isn't on the deck!"

"Yes," I said, and even though I was anxious to get upstairs, *ah topside*, I corrected myself, and take a good look around, I was a little disappointed that I hadn't been able to spend more time with Cat. She was so informative and she made me laugh. Plus I really wanted to know what she'd meant by that earlier comment when she mentioned Slade telling her and Patty that he didn't think I knew about boats.

Surely he hadn't been planning all along to take me on this trip. Could he have been looking for me at Lum's? I shook my head at such a thought. *Really*, I said to myself, *Cat is just confused... or maybe she's teasing me?*

"Hey, where's my drink?" Slade stood in the hatchway once again. I had started up the stairs and stopped when I tried to figure out what Cat's comment really meant.

"Oh, sorry," I mumbled as I continued up the stairs. The boat was lunging and I was unsteady. Slade reached out to take a drink from my hand then steadied me with a firm grip on my forearm.

The wind hit my face as I looked to the front—*ah, bow*—of the boat and marveled at the speed, the rush and swoosh of passing water. I breathed a deep breath and my lungs nearly exploded as more air was forced into them. My mouth felt dry.

"Hey, sit here." Slade was patting a cushion beside his.

"Oh my," I thought and was embarrassed when I realized that I'd said it aloud. I was totally out of my element and overwhelmed by everything that I was experiencing. "So this is life!" I said and this time I was careful to keep my thoughts to myself.

"A toast!" yelled Cat above the wind and clanging rigging.

"Prepare to jibe!" yelled Patty.

"What?" I asked, but in the midst of everything, Patty yelled again, "Jibe Ho!"

Slade grabbed my arm, pushed my head down, and directed me to the other side of the boat. Patty pushed at the wheel until it made at least a complete circle; Cat was now sitting where Slade had been a moment before. Sometime during all the commotion, I thought I heard a freight train and the boom came flying across the cockpit. Suddenly the seats were on the opposite side of the boat and we were turned around. Patty took a moment to trim the sails.

Now, we were once again in harmony with the sea and wind. The boat glided along the water, cutting a straight and narrow swath. The sails were full and happy. "To sailing!"

I tried to catch my breath as everyone else raised their glasses to Paddy's toast. I was too late to join in the toast, but I raised my glass and quickly drank to this wonderful sport.

To myself, I thought I'd always like to sail—or at least be on the water. This experience would change my life forever. Quickly, I reminded myself of the plan I'd made in the attic of my parents' house when I'd reached for the dangling wire. I nodded my head in acknowledgement—my remaining time on this good earth would include a great deal of life on the water. I could leave this world happily if I had such time on the sea.

CHAPTER TWELVE

For the next few days, we spent our time exploring small coves and sailing along the lengths of many islands. The weather was too beautiful to be believed and every day was a fantasy come true.

It turned out that we were a most compatible group. We actually spent so much time in one another's company that Slade and I spent little time alone. Even when we moored the boat and took the small inflatable to shore to visit island shops, we went as a cohesive group. Sometimes we'd lunch in one of the places that excelled at conch chowder, Patty's particular favorite, and spend hours drinking Bahama Mamas while laughing and talking and simply enjoying life.

This whole trip was a revelation for me. I never in my wildest dreams knew that such a way of life existed. I thoroughly enjoyed the casual days and the relaxing way that my companions and I pursued them. I did believe that if I died tomorrow, I would have been satisfied with my life.

When we were on the boat, we took turns making meals and cleaning up. No one complained and everyone, it seemed, did more than their share. In this environment, nothing was like the real work I'd spent a lifetime doing. I learned more about sailing, the boat itself, and I got an entire course from Patty, Bish, and Slade about emergency drills. Of course, no one expected that we'd be in need of evacuation or radioing for help, but I was given an accelerated course in all of the attendant procedures.

We sailed the course that Patty had laid out on the navigator's table, off the salon. It was a practical course giving us a lot of smooth sailing and time to enjoy the feel of earth under our feet. For the most part we stayed close to the protection of the islands' shores while avoiding the many reefs in the area. We also moored inside harbors every night for protection from any weather that might come up as well as the real danger of pirates attacking us and taking our belongings.

We ran half-naked on empty beaches feeling the sand so fine that it felt like confectioner's sugar under our feet. The first time I set foot on it I squealed with delight when it squeaked as I walked.

Each night we returned to the boat and often enjoyed a nightcap in the cockpit. We preferred to stay outside, admiring the moon on the water, the gentle breeze as we sipped our drinks and told stories. But when the breeze deserted us and our bug repellent failed, we'd retire to the safety of the stateroom. After our evening ritual, Paddy and Bish would head to their cabin in the stern and Slade and I would go forward to our berths.

I soon found that I'd wasted my time worrying about Slade or what would happen when we were quartered together. He was a perfect gentleman in all respects and was actually becoming more like the brother I never had. I was able to relax and not put much emphasis on the man-woman thing. Yet, sometimes I'd smile to myself in the darkness because I'd recall a moment when I caught him looking at me in a special way—or I'd remember how he'd take my hand while walking behind Paddy and Bish on an island excursion. Although I had moments of wondering if he had any feelings for me, I was, for the most part, grateful for this time where we could be ourselves, get to know one another as though we had all the time in the world.

As I lay looking through the porthole at the stars and magnificent sky, I pulled the light sheet about my shoulders and sighed.

"What are you thinking about?" Slade asked from his berth.

"About how lucky we are," I answered and waited for him to agree or make another comment. Soon I heard his soft snoring and knew that he was asleep. I smiled at the comfort of his nearness.

I was exhausted but found myself so excited about tomorrow's plans, I could hardly force myself to think about getting some sleep. Tomorrow was going to be a wonderful day. We'd planned a brunch-picnic on the shore at Abaco and then in the afternoon we were going shopping. Paddy and Bish were meeting friends they knew on the island and Slade and I had elected to spend some time entirely by ourselves.

I thought maybe we could find a beach cabana and spend our afternoon drinking Bahama Mamas, sitting on the creamy sand and running in the surf. The thought of the surf gave me a momentary chill as I remembered how Paddy had yelled for all of us to get out of the water the last time we'd played in the surf—seems he'd seen a small shark and a good-sized barracuda. I also found myself thinking about the day we'd thrown an anchor out and, barely in sight of land, we all jumped off the boat and went swimming. That was the day that Patty got stung by the man-o-war.

I concentrated on getting the sight of those big, red welts all over Patty's arms and chest out of my mind. My last conscious thought was of how easily we can forget the unpleasant things in life. Until now I'd forgotten the shark and barracuda sighting, as well as Patty's nasty encounter with the red jellyfish tentacles. I'd forgotten, too, about Patty and Cat's stories of the modern day pirates roaming these waters in jet boats, carrying automatic weapons and searching for people like us. Modern day pirates were far more ruthless than their predecessors—they didn't leave eyewitnesses and they never took prisoners.

CHAPTER THIRTEEN

I awoke suddenly, aware of noise and voices somewhere beyond my cabin door. "Slade, what's going on?" I whispered as I rolled over to face his berth.

"Slade?" I inquired as I tried to open my eyes. "What's happening?"

I stared at his empty berth, already made up with neatly folded swimming trunks, polo shirt and other clothing atop the spare blanket at the foot of the berth. I looked at my watch.

"Yikes, nine-thirty!" I gasped, as I realized how late I'd slept.

I fairly leapt off the berth and quickly began to get myself together. Once, I paused to listen to Slade, Bish and Paddy happily going about their business in the galley. I couldn't make out what they were saying but could hear them chatting back and forth, their conversation punctuated by laughter. I couldn't get over how natural I felt being on this boat with these people who'd been total strangers a week ago. I smiled at my happiness—I really didn't deserve it.

I slipped into the head unnoticed and when I returned to my cabin everyone had gone up on deck—the galley and salon were deserted. I wanted to join my friends. Quickly, I checked my purse to see that I had money, etc. and threw some clothes, sandals, suntan lotion, moisturizer and other essential items into the duffle where I kept my brooch. With what was now habit, I checked the sanitary napkin reassuring myself that the beautiful family pin was still safely inside. I didn't go anywhere without it. Satisfied that all was in order, I gave a last look around at the now-tidied cabin and headed for the deck to be with my friends.

Today was going to be so special I could hardly wait for it to begin. I looked forward to my time with Slade. I had a feeling that spending time with him alone would allow me to learn about his mysterious past, if I dared venture into that unchartered territory.

I felt giddy and slightly out of control like I vaguely remember being once or twice when I was a young girl in love. It was one of those rare moments in life when you just knew instinctively you were going to make memories. Somehow I was aware that this would be an unforgettable day in my life, that for however long I lived I would reflect on it and be thankful. Everything about this day would be perfect, I just knew it and therefore I wanted it to pass slowly so I could allow myself time to savor every precious second. I knew that in any case, life would be measured in a matter of months, not years. It was that decision that was responsible for my being here in the first place. As far as I was concerned, I had made the right choice and I wouldn't have traded a day of this trip for endless years alone on an Ohio truck farm.

Dressed in a white tank top and baggy blue shorts with new white sneakers, I fairly bounded through the cabin door.

On my way through the galley, I could hear Bish call to me.

"Evie, are you finally up?" she laughed.

"Yes, finally," I responded as I made my way up the galley steps and poked my head into the bright sunshine.

"Whoa, Sleeping Beauty, get your breakfast and join us. Hot, buttered French Toast in the oven, syrup on the counter, but I already sprinkled some confectioner's sugar on it...."

The rest of her words were lost on me as I opened the oven door and removed the plate, careful to use the oven mitts hanging neatly by the stove. I replaced one mitt, turned the oven off and carried my breakfast plate with silverware up the stairs and onto the deck where the others were waiting. I suddenly realized I was ravenous.

"Good morning," everyone greeted me in unison.

"Gosh, this is heavenly," I couldn't ignore the water sparkling like a million polished diamonds as the sun shone on it and the whisper of a breeze gently caressed the surface.

What a moment, I thought, moved by the beauty around me. I didn't remember experiencing anything like this in my life. I felt overwhelmed by everything.

These warm and generous friends, the absolute perfection of nature in harmony with the most beautiful boat imaginable... well, it was something all right.

I couldn't really describe it and do it justice, I thought.

I wanted to freeze this moment. I wanted to be able to call it up at will and bask in the...

"Excuse me," my thoughts were interrupted by Patty who was speaking to me. "Oh, Evie, it's so nice to see that you appreciate this as much as Bish and I do. We love this and in all our years on the water, we've never grown tired or bored with it. We love to see others enjoy it as much as we do."

"Umm;" agreed Slade, who, I thought was unusually quiet this morning.

For a moment I wondered what was occupying him but then I was overcome by hunger and the smell of the French Toast on the plate I still held in my hand. I got settled and busied myself with eating—the food was exquisite as always.

I was dimly aware of Bish and Paddy making small talk and laughing together. Once, I glanced up and saw them sipping their Mimosas—champagne and orange juice, I'd come to learn on this trip. Slade seemed lost in his thoughts still, quiet and introspective. I, too, remained silent, content with this paradise.

"Would you care for some more?" Bish asked, seeing my empty plate.

"Oh, ah, no, that was wonderful though!"

"Community effort," Slade spoke at last.

"Oh, yeah, Evie, you should have seen us. I'm surprised we didn't wake you with all the noise!" Bish laughed.

I found myself embarrassed at my oversleeping. I couldn't believe I'd done it as excited as I was about today. But then I had awakened at some point and tossed and turned for some time before I could relax and get back to sleep.

"I'll clean up," I volunteered and stood to gather the dishes.

"Hey, hold on. No hurry, you know. Why you haven't even touched your Mimosa!" Paddy exclaimed in mock horror.

"Oh, somehow I didn't think it would be that compatible with the French Toast and I didn't want to forego that treat."

"Well, nobody else had that problem or concern, I guess. We're on our third one and we had breakfast with the first…."

Paddy had spoken, but they all laughed heartily.

Somehow the beverage was still nicely chilled and there was a strawberry and orange slice perched neatly on the side of the glass.

I raised the glass, "To another glorious day!" I toasted.

"Here, here!" came the responses.

We raised our glasses higher and drank as one.

I picked the fruit from the side of my glass and nibbled it between sips. The drinks were cool and refreshing, in welcome contrast to the warm morning rays blanketing us. Each of us looked forward to the day ahead, but for some reason no one made a move to go ashore. By silent agreement we lounged, talked comfortably, made another pitcher of Mimosas savoring the company as well as the lusty drinks. It was as if we knew this would be our last day together.

Once, I looked at Slade; he seemed relaxed, staring off into space, a million miles away. I was struck again by his physical perfection, the sheer beauty of him. I reminded myself that he was still very much a mystery to me and for a moment I resolved not to get more involved with him until I knew much more about him—his past, his beliefs, practices, the core of his being. But deep down, I knew it was already too late for practical thinking, I realized I'd been lost to him when I first laid eyes on him in New York. I didn't know then whether or not I'd ever see him again but something had told me he was my destiny. I figured then that it was just wishful thinking on my part, but here we were....

With effort, I tore my eyes from him and glanced at Paddy and Bish. They were quiet now, gazing into each other's eyes and smiling. The reflection of the water caused the sunlight to dance on their faces giving the effect of a thousand butterflies suddenly set free. Their bare feet caressed one another's legs, their hands supported them and held their mimosas. From time-to-time, they sipped the magic juice, their actions in perfect harmony. How I enjoyed watching them and envied their happiness but now I felt like an intruder and I swept my eyes away.

Once again I thought about the trip to shore and time alone with Slade Williams. As anxious as I'd been for that time to arrive I found that in reality, I was happy in this place with these people and could be for the rest of my life—that somehow seemed to be a revelation for me.

I thought briefly of my plan, the brooch tucked securely in my bag and I smiled to myself. Yes, I'd come a long way. I'd learned much and I could die happy right now—satisfied. *At last I've lived, not necessarily as I'd imagined but it was enough, more than enough,* I thought.

We were startled out of our reverie by a passing sail boat.

"Ahoy, maties," two voices chorused simultaneously. It was obvious that they'd done this before.

"Beautiful day," they added.

Paddy yelled back, "Yeah, it's a beauty all right."

The rest of us smiled and waved as they sailed slowly away. The interruption had been brief but it was enough to alter the general mood. Still when a breeze attempted to blow a paper napkin overboard, it took a minute to respond. It was Bish that finally grabbed the thing before it floated over the side.

"Ah well," said Slade, "since we're all awake now, why don't we get going and see what else we can make of this gorgeous day." It was more a statement than question. Suddenly we were all inspired and moving about. Dishes were gathered, hastily rinsed and stacked. The kitchen gear was stowed and personal articles gathered for the day ashore. From nowhere appeared a large straw basket, square with a peg that locked two pieces of leather strapping securing the lid. It was the size of a small suitcase. Slade picked it up, smiled at me, but said nothing as we finished our preparations for the day trip.

Soon, the four of us were in our runabout heading for shore. No one thought anything about our not seeing any activity or so much as another boat in the quiet little cove where we'd anchored the beautiful Bristol.

I glanced back at the *Victoria E.* as she-lay contentedly on her anchor. She was majestic, dark and serene, a sea queen, royalty, in her own right. I marveled at what she represented for me, the fun, freedom, learning about the water and how to sail. She had become my sanctuary and more, difficult though it was to put into words, difficult too because it was temporary for me. I just couldn't imagine what it must be like to own a boat like that—I simply couldn't.

Once again I caught myself smiling at my pleasure and once again I felt guilty. I looked up to see what the others were doing and was taken aback to find they were all looking at me.

"Caught me," I groaned, embarrassed nearly to tears. My face was flushed. What must they think of someone openly gloating at their happiness. Still, I could feel the color rising on my neck and face, a deeper shade, and I knew it had nothing to do with the rays of the sun. At that moment, I did want to die.

Everyone was speaking at once—trying to assure me that they all knew how I felt. They told me they felt the same way and I shouldn't be embarrassed at all. Actually, they said, it was quite a compliment to them that I so enjoyed them, the boat, etc. They were so sweet to try and make me feel better. If only they'd known me a short time ago—if possible, my color deepened at the thought. I'd never shared the reason for my trip with these dear people, not wishing to taint their impression of me or dampen their natural enthusiasm and obvious joy in living. I had shown them the brooch but told them only that it was a family heirloom I dared not leave behind.

In the midst of my discomfort, I heard the engine stop and watched as Paddy skillfully lifted and turned the small motor to lock it into place. The boat slid gently into the sandy beach and Cat was up and out, bowline in hand, expertly pulling us up and into the higher sand area. The rest of us followed suit, laughing and splashing in the warm, perfect Caribbean. Slade and I were on one side of the boat, Bish on the other toward the bow. We pulled the boat well up on the shore lest the tide come in and take her out to sea. Our runabout was our transportation to and from the big boat and we were not going to take any chances that we would lose her. We plucked our respective belongings from the small craft now securely beached, and trudged along hurriedly to a nearby path, the confection-of-sugar sand hot on our bare feet. Cat nodded with familiarity at a sign nailed to an old tree. The sign was really several pieces of driftwood pointing in different directions inland. I squinted against the bright sun to read the hand-painted lettering on the driftwood. The names meant nothing to me but I was captivated by the effect of the white paint on the hand-picked driftwood. It was simple, quaint and very appealing to me.

Wordlessly, we copied Cat as she wiped her now dry feet on the grassy side of the path and brushed off the remaining fine grains of sand. She dropped the flip flops she'd held loosely in one hand and slid her feet into them. She turned, checked to see that the rest of us had also donned sandals or other shoes, nodded her satisfaction that we were shorn and could proceed. Without a word she turned back around and started down the path. We followed blindly, eager to enjoy yet another aspect of this grand adventure.

In no time we were poking our heads from the foliage and found ourselves at another beach—longer, this one seemed endless. From where we exited the path there was a huge cabana made out of a combination of wood and fronds with bamboo artfully applied here and there. A bartender who alternately whistled or hummed was enclosed in a horseshoe-style bar. Patrons in various states of beach and casual attire sat or stood around the outside of the horseshoe. The bar was quite populated and most of the tall bamboo stools were taken.

I could hear a steel band playing nearby and it was to this music that the bartender worked and hummed or whistled. My eyes followed in the direction the music seemed to be coming from and in the distance I thought I could make out the source. There was a large, elegant white building with wide porches that must have been where the band was stationed.

There were several couples walking from what appeared to be a hotel and the beach bar or cabana where we stood. It seemed to make sense that this actually belonged to the hotel.

Once again in silent communication, we followed Cat as she stepped onto the wide sand-filled staircase and up onto the floor around the horseshoe. Paddy was in front of Slade and me and he motioned us forward. I was surprised to see four empty barstools at the very tip of the "shoe". Cat was already seated and the rest of us quickly joined her. The bartender was busy with several blenders full of different colored froth but he didn't miss our arrival. With a huge smile he acknowledged our presence.

"Be right with you," he said and at the same instant a dish of some kind of nuts magically appeared on the bar before us.

The man was a model of efficiency—humming, smiling, greeting, serving, mixing—and still managing to make small talk with several of the customers. And, certainly everyone seemed happy and relaxed.

Paddy reached for the plastic beverage menu in front of him. "No hurry," he said as the bartender reached for another bottle of dark rum on the shelf on the rear wall.

"Paddy glanced at the drink list, smiled, and handed it to Cat, who also looked at it briefly and passed it to me. I studied the exotic names, "Volcano Bowl", "The Scorpion", "Pirates' Treasure", "Golden Dream", on and on the list went. The titles were in bold print and there was a brief description of each drink's contents but I had no idea what I wanted. I shrugged my shoulders, shook my head and passed the menu to Slade who looked at the list and then back at me.

"May I order for you?" asked Slade.

I nodded, relieved. I was quite sure that I'd probably enjoy whatever I got, but there were too many unfamiliar choices for me.

On the outside of the ends of the 'shoe' I could just make out an artist's rendering of a loin-clothed native on the side near us and a long-haired beauty in a sarong on the other. I stood and excused myself to make a visit to the ladies room.

"Wait for me," I heard Cat say behind me. I turned and waited, watching as she bent over and whispered something in Paddy's ear. He smiled and nodded; she gave him a light kiss on the cheek and walked toward me.

"My drink order," she explained when she'd caught up to me.

We walked together to the far end of the horseshoe where the ladies room was clearly marked below the picture of the native woman in the sarong.

We entered the room and squeezed past a woman who was on her way out. The room was clean and neatly appointed and we had it all to ourselves. Bish smiled a devilish grin. "So," she said, "do you think you and Slade can occupy yourselves around here for the rest of the day? The farther away from the hotel you get, the more private the beach...." She didn't finish the thought—just let her words hang in the air as she pretended to fix her hair. She winked at me in the mirror.

I smiled back at her. She was so adorable and truly a nice person. I disappeared into the stall, still smiling. I thought I was lucky to have found this extraordinary girl. I knew I had found a lifelong friend in her.

Cat was still standing next to the basins but took a step back as I emerged from the stall and walked to the sink to wash my hands.

"If I really make an effort, I think we can manage to amuse ourselves for a few hours," I said trying to keep a straight face and any trace of excitement out of my voice. Once again Bish looked into the mirror and straight at me. I could feel my face flush as she looked at me intently. I knew Cat was well aware that I hoped our time alone together today would help us know one another better and resolve some of the confusion of our feelings for one another. It was quite possible that we would find there was a friendship and nothing more but I found that hard to believe.

I couldn't help smiling as I slid into the seat next to Slade. There on the bar before us were two tall CC & Gingers.

I picked up my glass and took a big sip. The icy liquid slid down my throat, so pure and refreshing after all the fruity concoctions we'd ingested lately. I realized I was thinking about the lounge in New York and the first time I'd met the man who'd introduced me to this drink. My heart was pounding.

Paddy, Cat, Slade and I chatted comfortable and then suddenly Cat and Paddy were getting off their stools, empty Bahama Mamas on the bar before them. They checked their watches at the same time.

"How 'bout we meet right here at six and that way we can wander up to the hotel together and have a bite before returning to the boat," Paddy asked.

"Sounds fine to me," Slade said and looked at me for confirmation. I nodded in agreement and glanced at my watch, mentally calculating how much time Slade and I would have alone together.

Four glorious hours of us, I thought and wondered whether I was more excited about the prospect of having his company to myself than I was about the actual experience.

Lost to my thoughts, I was immediately returned to reality when I felt Slade's touch on my arm. I felt the goose bumps rise immediately.

Damn, I thought to myself, *it just wasn't fair that anyone could have this kind of effect on me!*

I was dimly aware that Slade was speaking to me.

"Huh," I managed stupidly.

"Penny for your thoughts?" Slade's sparkling eyes were searching mine.

Once again I could feel color rising from my neck to my face. His intense gaze still rendered me helpless. With difficulty I turned toward the bar and picked up my drink, nearly forgotten in the last few minutes. I took what I hoped were casual sips, trying to put my fire out and gain some control of my growing feelings. I knew I was being disarmed.

I looked toward the cabana opening leading to the beach or the path to the hotel. Bish and Paddy were long gone, of course, and Slade and I were very much alone. "I'm sorry," I finally replied. "I missed what you said".

"A penny for your thoughts," he repeated patiently.

"Oh not that," I smiled. "Whatever you said when I was daydreaming." I had hoped the vague response would satisfy him and he would not insist on knowing what I was thinking.

"Oh, I was asking if you wanted to find a nice spot on the beach and have something to eat—our picnic, remember?" he added playfully.

I was still full from the breakfast and doubted that I could touch food, let alone eat it with him sitting near me, staring at me, talking softly and touching my arm from time-to-time as he made a particular point or sought to get my attention.

NO, I was definitely not hungry for food and then I realized I was suddenly very nervous. I swallowed with some difficulty and not trusting my voice, I just nodded my head and smiled gamely.

I noticed Slade putting some bills on the bar and realized that our drinks were empty. Gallantly he took my hand and helped me from the stool. I had a quick flashback to our meeting at Lums in Nassau and groaned inwardly at how clumsy and inept I was then. I was shocked that in all the time we'd spent on the boat together, I had no more composure in his presence. I was still overwhelmed by him and the worst part of that was it seemed to be beyond my control. My own body betrayed me at any opportunity. Lamely I put my fingers to the front of my neck wondering if it were covered with hives like it was at Lums.

I picked up my tote bag and followed Slade. I realized I was fast becoming quite miserable at the prospect of spending four hours with this damn disarming individual who never seemed to say or do a wrong thing. I missed Bish and Paddy, their light and lively conversation and company had been a buffer allowing me to relax and find myself in this new life.

But I had to remind myself that I was living. I was experiencing what life had kept to itself all the long years I'd existed in Ohio. I trudged after Slade and almost ran into his back when he stopped suddenly to remove his sandals. I did the same. He smiled, picked up the basket and his sack and moved on.

Once or twice I glanced behind me, noting I could barely see the rather large cabana we'd left. I couldn't see the water faucet and steps on the edge of the beach that lead to it.

I shrugged my shoulders resigning myself to getting through this without too much embarrassment, I hoped. And I nearly laughed out loud at the ridiculous nature of my problem. Most girls would give an arm and leg to be in my shoes at this moment. Second, I was here solely to live and experience all that I'd missed. I surely had nothing to lose and this had the potential to be the best experience of my new life—however short-lived it turned out to be.

CHAPTER FOURTEEN

My feet felt like they were walking on clouds. With renewed vigor and determination, I followed Slade, making a game of trying to walk in his footprints without stepping on his heels. I felt like a child, unencumbered, excited, with boundless energy.

At last Slade slowed and turned to me with a question. I was lost in my thoughts, letting my mind wander and dance and found myself face-to-face with him.

"What?" I said brightly.

He stared at me for a moment, his eyes searching my face and quickly bent and placed a light kiss on my forehead. I was dumbfounded by this action and its spontaneity. I took a step back even as I contemplated reaching for his broad shoulders and pulling him closer. I lost my balance and landed in the sand at his feet, looking up at his face.

He burst out laughing as he bent toward me and his laughter was so infectious that I joined in forgetting to be embarrassed by my clumsiness around him.

Finally he caught his breath, took a long look around at

the vegetation behind us, the sparkling water in front of us and empty beach to our right and left.

"Perfect, don't you think?" he asked, smiling at me as he put the picnic basket down and sank into the sand beside me.

I nodded in agreement, kicked off my sandals and began rummaging through my tote for towel and lotion. Slade was busy in the picnic basket as I settled myself. The lid was between us so I couldn't see just what was in this mysterious picnic basket. He dug through the contents like he was going through a treasure chest. For a moment I wondered if he'd packed the basket himself or someone else like Bish had helped him. I smiled at him even though he was so focused on his task he didn't notice.

"Ah ha," he said in triumph as he pulled out a plastic container and two sealed plastic bags. I found that I was suddenly ravenous and was glad for the distraction of our picnic lunch.

Carefully, Slade spread a flexible straw placemat between us and uncovered the plastic container which must have held about three dozen small smoked oysters—a recent discovery of mine—in oil. Next, he placed the plastic bags on the mat and withdrew a large Chinette plate. I watched as he artfully arranged the Triscuits and sharp cheese from the plastic bags around the oysters. Finally, he withdrew a small cylinder which held fork-like hors d'oeuvre picks and then he removed a large thermos full to the brim with something. I looked at the condensation on the side of the thermos and wondered what concoction was within. At the same time I marveled that he'd taken time to prepare all this so early in the morning and considered how heavy this basket must be to lug around.

This was the most wonderful and thoughtful thing that anyone had ever done for me. I was filled with gratitude and warm feelings for this handsome mystery-man beside me. It was unbelievable to me that such a man could be so thoughtful and romantic—somehow it just didn't seem to fit....

Well, I determined not to concern myself with asking questions I couldn't yet answer. I was going to have the best damn day of my life and nothing less!

"What's in the jug?" I asked, pointing to the thermos, hungry, thirsty and so damn excited I could barely contain my joy. How was I going to sit still and eat and drink and carry on a conversation with this man who so unsettled me?

"My magic potion, guaranteed to enhance even the most perfect day," he replied softly.

You and your potions, I thought recalling how he'd gotten his nickname. But I said nothing as I didn't trust myself.

He removed two hard plastic glasses from the basket. It looked as though they'd been painted with every color in the rainbow—streamers and confetti of various shapes, lengths, sizes. I took the festive glasses as he held them to me and he proceeded to unscrew the wide top from the jug. I leaned forward unable to hide my curiosity.

Inside the jug was a deep scarlet liquid with "dyed" fruit slices dancing on the surface near the rim. I watched in fascination as he poured one glass then the other. A large orange slice escaped the container and plunked onto the full glass sending some of the red potion flying.

A few drops landed on my cheek and I put my index finger up and collected them, then licked my finger.

"Yum!" I couldn't help exclaiming. "What is this, really?"

"My own version of Sangria...full recipe when I know you better," he said with a chuckle.

I shook my head at him then drank deeply.

"Wow. This is truly fabulous—like an explosion of flavor and cold and refreshing." I groped to find the right adjectives to describe what I experienced. "Delicious and thirst-quenching," I added needlessly.

Holding an orange slice to the side, I finished my drink and held it out to Slade for a refill.

He was staring at me with a bemused expression on his face. His tanned features were slightly reddened as he sat facing the sun.

Was it possible he could be any more gorgeous, I thought, once again awed by the physical beauty of him. I couldn't yet believe that he wanted to spend his time with me, plain and dull as I was. I pushed that thought aside and lamely attempted some levity.

"Sorry, it evaporated, I think," I said half to myself.

"Yes, that happens in sun like this. But beware, this juice is deceptive. It can fell without warning," he added in an ominously odd tone.

I took another gulp and promised myself I'd sip from now on no matter how difficult.

Slade and I munched the oysters, crackers and perfectly chilled cheese and talked about the beauty of the islands we'd passed, the clarity and warmth of the surrounding waters. We talked about Bish and Patty and what a unique and daring lifestyle they enjoyed—fun, carefree and very appealing if you knew your way around a boat and these tricky waters.

We talked about some of his other friends and Hilly, Mary and Dan whom he'd met and liked.

Despite my resolution, I filled my glass again and again.

106

I had an overwhelming feeling of peace and well-being, running my toes through the sand, warmed by the sun's caress in easy conversation with Slade.

Suddenly, I was overcome with the urge to get to the water. I set my empty glass down and pushed it into the sand to keep it from tipping over. I arose slowly, careful not to kick any sand onto the nearly empty party plate.

"Going for a swim?" asked Slade, surprise evident in his voice.

"Just wading, I think. Wanna join me?"

Slade answered by getting up and grasping my hand. He began to run toward the water and I had no choice but to do the same. His grip was firm and natural as if our hands were meant to be joined in this way.

He slowed as we neared the water's edge and we stepped as one into the lukewarm water. We stopped when I was standing shin deep and I bent and splashed the water to my face and onto my bare arms. The gentle, balmy breeze that I'd not noticed before dried me instantly so I repeated the act.

Slade was watching me intently. With purpose he reached for me and with his arm around me and one hand in the small of my back, he pulled me toward him. His action took me completely by surprise and I didn't have time to think of a response. He held me close and bent down and kissed me passionately. His wine-sweetened mouth made me think I was kissing some kind of god.

I had a floating sensation and didn't know if it was due to the wind, the sun or the heady emotions I was experiencing for the first time in my life. I could feel Slade's strong arms tightening around me and I was grateful for the support. My knees were so weak I felt I would slip below the surface of the water and float away.

"I wish we could stay like this forever," Slade whispered in my ear.

"Ummmm," I concurred from my dream-like state.

"But Bish and Paddy will be waiting for us by now."

His words shocked me out of my reverie. I moved my arm to where I could see my watch.

"My God," I said, shocked that it was so late and I was so disappointed that we had to leave at this point. I couldn't believe it was so late,

"Where did the day go?" I asked myself.

I hadn't realized it but the water was at the hem of my shorts. With effort, I made my way to shore.

"I don't believe this!" I exclaimed again, but under my breath. I laughed at myself—all my fears, plans of yesterday—I needn't have worried as it turned out. I found that I felt cheated somehow.

Slade and I hurriedly pulled ourselves and belongings together. Hastily we headed back down the beach to the Cabana to meet our companions. What had recently transpired between us was pushed aside for the time being and now I wasn't sure whether or not I'd imagined the passion, the promise of intimacy....

I glanced at my watch as we stepped up and into the Cabana. It had taken us nearly half an hour to get to our picnic spot yet we'd made it back to the meeting point in half that time. Still, we were ten minutes late.

Paddy and Bish were occupying the same stools they'd had earlier. They were the only guests at the bar. When they saw us approaching they quickly got off their stools and came to us.

"I'm starved. Let's go directly to dinner and we can

have our cocktails while we wait to be served," Bish said in one breath.

"Okay," Slade and I chimed in together and we automatically followed our friends out the door and up the path. We hardly noticed the bartender wave goodbye as we departed.

The hotel was very lovely and even larger than it appeared from the Cabana. It must have been recently painted with the whitest white paint money could buy. The black shutters and trim were an old-fashioned but elegant contrast. It reminded me of the lovely Southern plantation mansion, Tara—something right out of *Gone With the Wind.*

The porch was filled with out-sized white wicker chairs with extra wide arm rests. Occasionally there was a hole in the wicker for a glass to be set into. There were a variety of wicker chairs, rocking and otherwise, set around the large porch. Here and there wicker flower holders with long stems and rounded bases held ivy or brilliant green moss and vine arrangements. The effect was subtle but startling. From the moment I stepped onto the porch I felt like I'd been transported back in time.

I was enthralled and began to walk around, feeling the atmosphere was at once enchanting but eerie. I noticed a movement just off the porch and saw a couple swinging in a large white slat and wicker swing.

"We can tour the veranda after dinner if you want," Bish interrupted my thoughts. I thought there was just a hint of impatience in her voice—not at all like Bish.

"Oh, okay," I said quickly, not wanting to keep her from eating since she and Paddy seemed to be starved. I felt full from all the Sangria, fruit, oyster crackers, and cheese I'd consumed. I doubted I could eat much now and would really have enjoyed just wandering around the grounds, experiencing my own thoughts about my feelings for Slade. But I felt Slade's arm encircle my waist and guide me through the massive double mahogany doors and into the main lobby of the hotel.

A handsome ebony gentleman in an immaculate white tux with a black bowtie bowed slightly, smiling. He greeted us as he glided to our group and motioned us forward as if he was the host inviting dear friends into dinner.

"Hotel, reservations?" he asked in perfect English. "Or drinks in the lounge before dinner?"

"We'd like to have drinks with our meal. Is there a wait?"

"Oh, no, I believe I could show you directly to a table where you may order immediately. As a matter of fact, I will take your drink order myself, how will that be?"

"Great!" Bish said, with obvious relief that dinner would not have to be postponed until after cocktails in the lounge.

"Right this way, then."

We were seated next to a large window in a cozy corner of the room. Abundant greenery and fresh cut flowers filled the room and the scent was heavenly without being overwhelming,

"I will take your drink orders now, if you're ready?" the handsome maitre-de said, suddenly brandishing pen and pad.

"Shall I order for you?" Slade inquired softly,

"Please do," I said, relieved. I had no idea what I wanted, if anything. I was beginning to experience a sense of uneasiness and couldn't pinpoint its origin.

I turned my attention to Bish and Paddy, who seemed uncharacteristically reserved. Bish was studying the menu intently and fidgeting with a napkin ring while Paddy kept glancing between Bish and the double doors we'd just entered. For a moment I wondered if perhaps the friends they'd visited in the afternoon were to join us but I wasn't comfortable asking. I stared at my hands in my lap. I stole a glance at Slade to see if I was imagining things or if he'd noticed a change in his friends. He was steadfastly looking at the menu.

Slade ordered appetizers of cold soup and shrimp for us. Paddy and Bish ordered large meals and at first seemed to have lost their appetites when the food arrived. But once they began eating, they ate heartily. There was little time for chit-chat and everyone concentrated on eating instead of socializing.

Dinner was long and tedious without the normal banter of our group. Finally it was over and we all had cream de menthe parfaits for dessert. Slade picked up the tab and we were on our way. Nobody mentioned walking around the veranda as we'd planned earlier and I decided not to bring it up now.

The night was comfortably warm and inviting with a huge, orange full moon shining above us. We had no problems getting back to the beach where we'd left the runabout.

I was vaguely aware of an eerie, uncomfortable feeling like I'd experienced back at the hotel. Now, it felt like I'd been transported from paradise into the twilight zone. I shivered involuntarily.

Once aboard the *Victoria E.* we did our respective chores securing the boat for the night. Slade and I took turns washing for bed and immediately retired forward. Neither of us spoke for several awkward moments. Each of us was under a sheet in the V-berth, facing the hull instead of toward one another.

My mind was reeling with unexamined feelings from this afternoon mixed with an urgent need for his explanation of how Bish and Paddy had acted since we met them for dinner.

While I waited for Slade to say something, I wondered what had happened to Paddy and Bish after they'd had drinks with us at the Cabana. Thinking back, that was the last time they'd seemed like themselves.

What could have caused them to be so serious, quiet and so out of character? I wondered.

"Good night, sweet lady. I had a wonderful afternoon on the beach with you. Thank you," Slade said politely.

For an instant I hesitated responding. I so much wanted to spend private time reliving my afternoon but as much as I wanted to reflect on my feelings for Slade and his for me, I was more concerned with what had happened between Paddy and Bish.

Had they fought, had a major disagreement, a bad experience—What?? Did they tell Slade? Did he have any thoughts of his own on what had transpired with them this afternoon? I was baffled and wanted to ask his opinion.

I rolled over to face him but his back was to me.

"Slade? Do you mind if I ask you something, ah, kind of, as, rather on the personal side, I guess?" I asked timidly.

"No, of course not," he said without hesitation and that immediate response heartened me. Then he added, "I don't have to answer you though…." And then he laughed softly.

Well, at least he hadn't changed, I thought with some reassurance and a measure of relief.

"Well, I ah, I just thought maybe I did something or said something or, oh, I don't know. Do you think Paddy and Bish acted upset this evening? Have you ever seen them so serious—so reserved? Do you think I angered or...."

"No," he cut me off mid-sentence. "I don't think it was anything to do with us." He said gallantly.

So he had noticed something unusual with their demeanor, I thought but decided to ask, "Have you ever seen them like that before?"

"Never," he replied without a moment's hesitation. "Something happened for sure," he added. "They didn't have their bags, knapsacks or anything with them when they returned to meet us for dinner. Did you notice that?"

"No!" I gasped, suddenly realizing Slade was right. "How could I have missed that," I wondered and then knew that I'd been just a little preoccupied because of the afternoon with Slade and all the Sangria and sun. I was embarrassed I'd been too muddled to notice such an obvious thing.

"What could have happened to their things?" I wondered aloud. "Should we go see them—see if they're okay now or if there's something we can do for them? Oh, my God, Slade, do you think someone robbed them?" I asked, aghast at the thought.

"Let's see what tomorrow brings—I'm sure a good night's sleep will do us all good and I know them—they'll tell us when they're ready, if they want to, that is...." his voice was patient and soothing but he added no more.

"Well, if they aren't acting normal tomorrow, I'd like to say something to them. They are so darling, so sweet, they've been so wonderful to me. I can't bear to think something bad had happened to them and there's nothing I can do to help or...."

"Yes, that's nice, dear. Let's see how things go in the morning. If they don't bring it up and they still seem like something's bothering them, you and I will talk then, okay?"

"Okay," I said. "Good Night, Slade." I would miss our usual evening banter tonight but I rolled over, resigned to get some sleep.

"Good night, dear lady."

CHAPTER FIFTEEN

I was barely conscious. I could hear the water lapping against the sides of the boat—close, so close. I tried to open my eyes—couldn't. It felt as if someone had sewn them shut during the night. The skin on my forehead was hot, stretched as tightly as a wound rubber band about to break.

Slade warned me about the Sangria headaches. "Worst in the world," he'd cautioned yesterday as I'd drunk the delicious concoction like it was water.

"Oh," I groaned, except it sounded more like a croaking sound than a groan.

Mentally I took inventory. Every part of my being hurt, ached and was on fire, pain so intense it made me want to throw up. It hurt to breathe; my God, even my teeth were killing me!

With every ounce of determination and strength I could summon, I forced myself to move. I opened one eye.

What? Where am I? my mind screamed in terror.

I was in a small boat, floating, bobbing along, no motor, no oars, no nothing.

No nothing! I repeated in my mind. I turned my head slowly, looking for something, someone else—anything....

I forced myself to look over the side of the skiff—this was our runabout I thought, though I knew I must be out of my mind. The pain was more unbearable with each passing moment.

God, I was dreaming—had to be. I had to wake up, to shake myself out of this state. What was wrong with me? I wondered if maybe I'd suffered a stroke—too much sun, Sangria yesterday? What? *Oh....*"

The sun beat down on me and the pain went beyond unbearable. I started to heave, dry heaves. My head felt like a mixture of thunder and strobe lights within. My mouth was dry and it felt like my stomach adhered to my backbone.

With effort, I reopened the only eye that seemed to work. I peered over the rail—only water, water everywhere.

"Everywhere?" I croaked in disbelief. "Everywhere?"

I opened my other eye slowly, looked forward and aft, checked out one side and then the other. Only the diamond-filled water sparkled in the strong sun and slight breeze—a breeze I couldn't feel on my own skin though feebly I raised one arm as though wanting to be called on to answer a question.

There was no doubt now. I was alone. I looked for my bag, my tote. What had happened? Where were my friends? Where was the *Victoria E.?*

In my damaged state, I looked again for my belongings. *Where was my brooch, my heirloom?*

I became aware of water sloshing around the floor of the runabout and looked down. The water was blood red and there were red and brown streaks staining the other seat and walls of the boat!

"Blood," I croaked and began to wretch in earnest. All the while my mind screamed, *My God, what's happened? Whose blood is that? Where is Slade? Paddy and Bish?*

There was no answer from the sea except the gentle rocking of the boat, the quiet lapping of the water outside, the sight sloshing noise around my feet.

I no longer had the strength to support my upper body and fell back on my elbows. I experienced more pain as the thin skin connected with the hard wood of the seat. The sounds became more distant, my vision blurred then darkened. I felt a sinking sensation and knew I was dying.

No! No! No! ...not like this—not now—not here! my mind screamed with rage and the injustice of it all. *No....*

CHAPTER SIXTEEN

I could hear voices, sense intense light and experience the sensation of movement. I didn't have to breathe. I didn't have to turn my head, yet I could see through the side of the wooden skiff. I could see sun-bright water, sense people sailing and having fun—boats under sail with big colorful spinnakers—and in the distance ships laden with cargo and low in the water plied their way to and from intended ports.

It was extraordinary, like the only sense I had was a blind sight. I felt no pain, smelled nothing, heard nothing except for this overwhelming, all-consuming sense of movement and the illusion of vision.

I believed my brain had somehow become disconnected from my body.

Am I disembodied? I asked myself and was amused at the thought. I thought of a lifetime past—my parents, old Bounder, the truck farm and rich soil along the banks of the Muskingham. Ah, the sweet, sweet earth yielding bountiful crops, the old family homestead with its heavy furniture and dozens of afghans made by long dead relations. I thought of the brooch, passed down from generation to generation. I felt sad when I realized I'd be the last of my line and the brooch was gone—lost, stolen?

Then I *saw* Mary, Hilly, Bill Tanner, the Drum Beat Club, my time in Nassau, the brooch again—I pushed it from my thoughts. I saw the chaperones without judgment, passion or pleasure. They were but bits and pieces of a running collage that came unbidden to my mind.

And finally Slade, Bish, Paddy, the *Victoria E.,* and then Slade again, looking at me with urgency in his eyes. I felt then, his hands on my shoulders shaking me. I knew it was terribly important to hear him, to do as he commanded but I could not hear, could not understand. And then with this last disturbing vision unlike the other fleeting images— the screen of my mind went blank and was unyielding. I wanted—no needed—to know about Slade and what he was doing, telling me, but there was no more.

And there I was—or was not—in a state like suspended animation for all eternity,

How odd, I thought but should not complain for I did not hurt, did not hunger, needed not to attend to bodily functions. I was not afraid or lonely.

Yes, I said to myself, *a very peculiar state indeed. What could it be?*

"Coma."

I heard the word clearly.

"Presented that way, oh…" papers rustled "…ten days ago."

Who said that? my brain wanted to know. *What kind of creatures spoke this way—'presented that way'—what the hell did that mean? What was happening? Where was I? How come I felt so strange? How…What…* Questions came

119

but nothing else.

"Yeah," the 'coma' voice continued, "...pirate attack in the Bahamas...as far as we know she's the only survivor, this Jane Doe. Found floating in a blood-spattered skiff—concussion, ah...closed head injury, internal injuries, battered and bruised but breathing—barely. No other information available, uhmm, no ID and was airlifted to us—well, to New York really, like this, comatose and unlikely to make it, but someone thought she should be given the opportunity so she came through our trauma unit—big bird brought her in but New York and Boston were fogged in so we're the lucky ones that get to explain it at mortality review..." continued the voice.

"Hey, she's holding her own...looks like. Anyway, she must have one hell of a story and I'd like to see her pull through. I wonder...." And the second voice trailed off. "Hasn't come to? Hasn't spoken?" the second voice again.

"No, not really. Once, we thought she was coming 'round. We were trying to assess the extent of the head trauma and getting set to do Burr Holes and she said something like, 'hilly, hilly, hilly.' That was that... lights out again, almost for good. She coded at the start of the procedure and again when we thought she was stable and Neuro attempted it again.

"Then there was some minor improvement and the brain swelling seemed to stabilize."

"Really?" the second voice again.

"Yeah, we were afraid she was going to cone but...."

"Excuse me, but I'm from the lab and I have to draw some blood. Should I come back?"

"No, no, come in. We're done here for the moment anyway."

"Doctor?"

"Yes?"

"Ah, what did you mean about the cone…that you were afraid she was going to cone?"

The doctor looked at the lab tech for a moment, noticed the blue M.T. (A.S.C.P.) patch—insignia of a registered medical technologist, college grad, 12 months training, boards. etc.…

"Coning is what happens when the brain swells and has nowhere to go. Basically, it expands into the spinal canal."

"And," the inquisitive med tech persisted.

"And," the doctor concluded, "it is fatal."

"Ah, ah, well thank you. I'd just never heard the term before." She began setting up for the phlebotomy. She checked her orders for blood work and withdrew the proper needle, tubes, wipes, gauze, and sterile bandaid. She checked my ID band and hospital number, grabbed the bulb on the blood pressure cuff to inflate as a tourniquet and started to pump it so she could palpate a vein.

"Hilly, Hilly, Hilly.…"

"Doctor, Doctor, she just said something," the med tech said aloud.

The doctor and the nurse were half way to the nurses' station, chart in hand but they were back in the room in an instant.

"What?" the doctor queried.

"Well, I'd inflated the cuff—ah, I was using it instead of a tourniquet—and she just mumbled something."

The doctor checked the pupils, then pinched the skin on the back of my hand without the IV.

"Odd," he said. "She charts negative for response to pain stimuli but seems to react to certain uncomfortable or painful procedures."

He pinched my arm and shook his head. "No, nothing," he said with a hint of disappointment in his voice.

"Carry on," he said as he and the nurse returned to the nurses' station and sat down to work on progress notes and write new orders, the tech noted and turned her attention back to the patient.

As she busied herself with the task of rechecking the Identaband to insure she had the right Jane Doe, she thought for a moment about this 'coning' thing and gave an involuntary shudder. Forcefully, she pushed the horrible image from her mind and once again inflated the BP cuff.

"Nice veins," she mumbled to herself. This was not often the case when someone in this shape had been in SCU for a while.

"Little stick," she said automatically as she inserted the needle and the blood began to flow into the Vacutainer tube. When she had what she needed, she simultaneously mixed the tube of blood and put it in the rack on the patient table. She withdrew the needle and began applying pressure to the puncture site. When she was satisfied the patient wouldn't bleed from the site, she folded a sterile gauze pad and placed it over the site and anchored it down with a bandaid. She then labeled the tube holding it next to the patient's arm band while copying the exact identification name, number, date, time, etc.

Satisfied everything was in order, she left the room.

"Thank you," came from the nurses' station, "Janet Rogers, MT (ASCP)" he added with a smile.

"Welcome," she called over her shoulder as she headed out of SCU to the nearby bank of elevators for personnel only. *Hmm,* she thought to herself, *Dr. M. Bouchard seemed very nice—very nice, indeed.*

Then added, *Jane Doe is in good hands.* She looked around the empty elevator and smiled as she thought of her encounter with the young doctor.

CHAPTER SEVENTEEN

I was in this half here–half not here state for what seemed like an eternity. I know I'd intended to gather my life experiences and be accepting that my life was over as long as I felt I had lived. This, however, was quite another matter. It was totally unacceptable and I still had much to do! First, I needed to find out what happened on the *Victoria E.* I had to find Bish, Paddy and Slade no matter what the cost time-wise or money-wise.

Money? Did I even have any? Time? Did I have that? How badly was I injured? What had happened? My mind asked over and over again like some tape playing in a continuous loop.

I could feel someone's presence in the room and then there was something thrust into my ear. Shortly afterwards, I felt pressure on my upper arm as the blood pressure cuff was inflated. For some reason I hated the sound of the rubber ball being pumped.

I opened my eyes.

"Welcome back," came a gentle, feminine voice.

My eyes were unable to focus immediately. I searched above me for the face that belonged to that welcoming voice.

Before I could see her, she said, "Excuse me, I'll be right back." And she gave my forearm a light squeeze and in a whoosh of white uniform departing, the room was quiet. I concentrated on how I felt. I assessed my arms and legs and head and the rest of me as best I could and concluded that I felt lousy actually.

"Well, say, this is a welcome surprise, young lady," a man's voice intoned.

The door to my small room closed as the room grew darker as someone drew a short drape across the glass in the window and door facing the nursing station.

Suddenly I heard a click and the room was flooded with bright light. "Ahhhh!" I cried out involuntarily.

"Cold cloth, please, Nancy," the man said and shortly afterward a cold compress was applied to my forehead and covered my aching eyes.

"There now, is that better? You gave us quite a run for our money," the doctor said kindly.

"I did?" I asked dumbly. My voice sounded harsh and raspy, my throat hurt and I sounded more like I was croaking than talking.

"Oh yes, but we'll get to that. We're just glad that you're awake now. I'm Doctor Autumn, a fourth year resident here. Now, if it's okay, we'll just look things over and see how you're mending. Would you like a sip of water first?" he asked.

"Oh, yes, please."

Gratefully, I took the bent plastic straw between my sore lips and drew a deep drink. It hurt to swallow but the cool liquid felt marvelous and I was so thirsty. I drank again.

"Easy, easy," said Dr. Autumn, "You'll have plenty of time to catch up," he assured me. Just take little sips for now. Okay?"

"Okay," I agreed. From that point, I was poked and palpated, the compress was lifted temporarily as a bright beam of light probed my one eye, then the other.

"Follow my finger," came the command.

I did as I was told but mostly I thought about the cruise, the beautiful, regal *Victoria E.,* and my friends Patty and Bish and, of course, Slade. And I felt a deep ache in my chest. I wondered and I worried how I would find them again. *What could have happened to us? Why?*

I could hear soft voices in the background and feel hands here and there on my head, my body. I responded when I was asked to lift a leg or given another direction but mostly I just thought about my last day in paradise and wondered what had followed.

My head began to throb and I groaned softly.

"Am I hurting you?"

"No, my head—it, it's splitting open."

"I'm not surprised it feels like it is but it's really in pretty good shape now," he added, "according to the latest CT Scan"

"Nurse, let's see if we can make her a little more comfortable. 75 mgs of Demerol and 25 mgs of Phenergan, please."

"Yes, Doctor. I'll get it right away."

"What's that Dem—Phena what?"

"Something for your head and an anti-nausea medication. We couldn't give you anything for pain before because of your head injury; we had to evaluate you first.

"Then, there was no need to worry about your pain

since you didn't seem to be in any discomfort. The less medication we gave you, the better we could assess what was going on."

"Here we are doctor," the nurse stated upon her return to the room.

"Oh, thank you, Nancy. Now, young lady, this will make you more comfortable."

"A shot!" I said, horrified at the prospect. "I just hate needles."

"Yes," Dr. Autumn laughed, "a shot."

I barely felt the injection.

"Okay now, Jane, we'll turn off the lights and refresh your cold compress. You relax and we'll be back later."

"But Doctor, I have questions. I need to talk to you. Where am I? How did I get here? How long have I been here? Where are my...."

"We have questions, too. You have obviously been through quite an ordeal and your body has been stressed to its limits medically. You are going to be just fine but right now, please try and relax—let the shot do its work and get some rest while your body continues to heal."

Then the pain lessened and a miraculous thing occurred: I was completely pain free. I felt terrific, like I was lighter than air—flying.

My God, what did he call that stuff? This was even better than CC and Ginger, I thought and laughed aloud.

How long had it been since I laughed? How long had I been here? Where was here? I was sure I was no longer in the Bahamas but where in Hell was I then?

Why did Dr. Autumn call me Jane?

I was struggling with these questions but my mind was fuzzy and I kept forgetting what I wanted to know and...I was so tired. All the tension had left my body. I slept for what felt like the first time in weeks —odd since I heard I'd been in a coma....

CHAPTER EIGHTEEN

"Good morning," the pleasant voice brought me to my senses. I'd been awake for some time but I lay quietly, thinking about what I was going to do. How was I going to pay for all this? How was I going to get back to Abaco to search for Patty, Bish and Slade? Had they even found the *Victoria E.* yet?

"Hi!" I responded, trying to sound just as bright and cheery.

After all, I reasoned. If I was in good shape, they'd send me home.

Home, I thought. *Well, maybe not home since I didn't have one but at least they'd let me leave.*

"When can I go home?" I asked in my healthiest voice.

"Oh, you'll have to ask your doctor about that. I'm from the lab, here to draw some blood for tests," she said matter-of-factly.

"Ah," I said, slightly embarrassed, "sorry."

"Oh, that's okay," she smiled. "I get asked that all the time...and worse," she added as she proceeded to busy herself with checking my name band and collecting the sample.

I cringed. I really did hate needles—always had, ever since I could remember. "You know," she said, smiling at me. "You look a lot better than you did yesterday!"

"I feel a lot better," I said and smiled back at her.

"Well, see ya. Glad you're feeling better," and then she was gone. The room was quiet once more.

All of a sudden there was a stir at the nurses' station and people started running toward me.

"CODE BLUE SCU II" came over the PA system. That thing had been chattering constantly in the background but this was the first time I actually heard it. People ran past me and into the room next door. I could hear carts banging into the bed rails.

"Get those side rails down," I heard clearly.

More white coats rushed past my room.

"No blood pressure."

Gosh, the walls were thin, I thought. I couldn't see anything but otherwise it was like I was in the room next door with that poor soul. And the smell was sickening. *What the hell was going on?*

"GI Bleed," I heard next.

"Call BB, Type and Cross, 8 units. Call Dr. Jacob's team in—alert the OR, we got a bleeder coming!"

Pandemonium—complete and utter chaos—or was it organized pandemonium? I wondered. I just couldn't stand it and the smell was awful. I was going to be sick!

I tried to get out of bed. I couldn't. I tried again but felt dizzy and had to lie back down. *How long has it been since I'd stood?* I wondered.

Well no matter, I had to get out of here. I couldn't stand it a minute longer! I felt a sharp pain in my temple but it passed and was replaced by a duller, more tolerable ache; my stomach hurt.

I swung my legs over the side of the bed where the lab girl had forgotten to return the railing to its raised position.

Oh my God, the catheter, I thought in horror as I looked down. No tube—no bag. It was there yesterday—when had it been removed? And the IVs, when did they take those out? And those things taped to my chest had disappeared as well. I didn't remember them doing all that—seems I'd lost track of things for a bit.

"Well, I don't have time to think of all that now. I'm on a mission," I said softly as I stood. On shaky, unsteady legs, I worked my way to the small closet. I held onto the bed, the tray table, some metal box on wheels in the middle of the room and from there to the closet. I leaned against the wall next to the closet, my strength exhausted.

But I was determined. I tried to calm my breathing, steady myself and then I opened the closet!

There on the hook were two cotton johnnies and I groaned, nearly defeated. I couldn't do this—what was I thinking?

But, I couldn't stay and I didn't want to. I had no answers to questions—I'd have to get those myself. I had no money—I'd have to figure a way to pay them later when I found my brooch, my money, my friends. I would have liked to learn what was wrong with me, where I was, how I got there, why I wasn't kept for treatment in the Bahamas, but that too would have to wait or go unanswered. What did it matter, anyway? *This certainly wasn't part of my Grand Plan.*

With some difficulty, I put one of the fresh johnnies on backwards so my rear end wasn't exposed and, on impulse,

I grabbed the robe and pulled it loosely across my shoulders. I used its belt to tie around my waist. Vaguely I realized that I now had a waist. I took a last look at the closet and saw something on the shelf—I reached for it. "It" was a pair of hospital socks, ankle high things with slip-proof treads on the soles- -ugly. I rerolled them and jammed them into my robe's pocket.

The floor was cold but somehow it made me feel alive, stimulated. I desperately needed to hold onto that sensation. I was so weak. I needed to focus on the cold floor and my pain to keep me moving. There was a hand rail that ran all along the wall and I held it tightly as I tried to center myself so I could move forward again.

The smell was worse, the noise was worse, a crush of white coats appeared outside my door along with the poor soul on the stretcher, IV poles right and left, and a box on wheels and various other pieces of medical equipment.

I could hear the person moaning and I gripped the hand rail that ran along the walls. I looked at the person on the stretcher. He was an elderly gentleman, I could see. He kept kicking up his legs, lifting the sheet, and I could see bright red blood spurting out of his bottom. He was covered with it and I turned my head. The smell was sickly-sweet and overpowering. His moans were growing louder and louder and I felt the walls closing in on me.

I followed the white-coated mass. It stopped outside the Special Care Unit by a bank of elevators, labeled "STAFF ONLY". I saw a hand reach out and press all three "UP" buttons as I kept going and rounded the corner. I was still very shaky and still using the hand rail and wall for support.

I wanted clothes; I wanted shoes, and I thought that a hospital would be pretty easy pickings since people shed their identities when they donned the open-backed hospital attire and footies. Shoes and clothes would be everywhere but I couldn't risk being caught and returned to that awful 'unit' and I didn't want to steal someone else's things— apparently mid-west ethics existed even in this predicament.

On the other side of the staff elevators were a bank marked, 'PUBLIC.' I looked around and to my surprise and relief, I saw no one. But I did see a sign marked, "EXIT" and after I put all my weight on the door handle, the heavy door gave way and I found myself in a deserted stairwell. I held tightly to the old wooden railing and carefully made my way down to the next floor. As I crept along, I was still thinking about finding some clothes and justifying my actions. I reasoned that I had nothing to lose; I was no longer playing by normal rules—not since I reached for the dangling wire in the attic of my parents' house; and failing to end it all then— my Grand Plan had been hatched. The time in between then and now had been mere months but felt like years.

Suddenly, I heard a door bang and voices above me coming down the stairs. Now, the clothes problem seemed trivial, the least of my concerns at the moment. I tried to increase the rate of my descent. Then the voices faded and disappeared altogether behind the bang of another door.

I was feeling rather poorly and quite done-in but I had to admit that this was a very exciting experience. I could easily say that I'd never found myself sneaking out of a hospital!

At last, I was near the bottom floor, I thought, as I looked inside to see if I was on the first or the ground floor... I wanted the least contact with others, the quickest, most direct way out. I couldn't see enough without opening the door wider so, with difficulty, I opened the crack a little wider. I saw signs with arrows directing people to: Admitting, Out Patient, Path

Lab and Coffee Shop. I closed the door as quickly as I could but noticed a flower cart being pushed toward me.

"Ahhhh," I didn't want to be caught. I reluctantly descended what looked to be the last flight of stairs. *God, I wondered, what was 1 likely to find here? The morgue?* I asked myself and shuddered at the idea.

With what seemed like my last ounce of strength, I cracked the door and peered inside. I found myself in a kind of cement tunnel, long and cold and eerily empty. This was like a different world—no brightly painted walls, or colored arrows helping visitors and patients to their destinations, no hustle or bustle, no carts, tray tables or stretchers lining the hallways. No, here there was nothing but silence and a sign at the end of the corridor that read, 'EXIT.' This became my immediate destination.

I opened the door wider and checked again before slipping inside the hallway. Once more, using the wall to steady myself, I shuffled along quietly, with total concentration. I was determined to succeed at this Great Escape, as I'd come to call it.

However just before the exit sign, there were several rooms, empty now, but who knew for how long? One room seemed to be an anteroom—it had no window, a small desk, shower and set of lockers. An antique coat rack stood in the far corner. I could see a white shirt on a hook and a suit coat jacket beside it.

Before I could think or stop myself, I stepped in and snatched the items. I could see a door with bright light coming from its window. I hurried into the hall, past the large double doors that housed the room with the bright light. AUTOPSY ROOM read the recessed sign over the door. I could see light coming from under the double doors which were on hinges and did not quite reach the floor.

"My God"— I was freezing all of a sudden. *Did I say that out loud?* I asked myself in horror. Without thinking, I glanced across at the double doors and saw a large metal door with a giant bolt on the outside. Beside it was a poorly lit narrow staircase leading upward. Really medieval—so different from everywhere else in the hospital.

I had to let go of the wall when I passed the double doors for fear of putting too much weight on them and ending up pushing them wide open, thereby exposing whatever horror lurked on the inside.

I was very grateful when I was able to use the wall for support once again but after another short distance I saw a third room on this side of the seemingly endless tunnel. This one had a door and it was open. There was a desk inside and a chair on wheels. Beneath the chair was a pair of dirty white high top basketball sneakers. I grabbed my socks from the pocket of the hospital-issue bath robe and shrugged it off my shoulders. I hung it on the hook I somehow knew would be on the back of the office door. Without hesitation, I put the white shirt on over the johnnies and belted it with the robe's belt. The shirt was huge! I set the suit coat on the desk for a second while I put the shoes on; they were filthy and too big. Quickly I grabbed the nonskid socks and put them on then reattached the sneakers to my feet—better. I picked the coat off the desk, knocking over a placard which I picked up and straightened—"Deanor," it read.

Deanor, odd name, I thought and moved on before Deanor returned.

In seconds I was out the door, standing at the top of a ramp in the beautiful sunshine. I was outside! There was a small parking lot with a couple of lined spaces beside the ramp and just off to the side a huge stack—possibly an incinerator of some sort....

I walked across the little parking lot, a narrow one-way street and found myself on the sidewalk of what appeared to be a run-down area of town. I saw a gigantic tenement house that looked condemned with boards on the broken windows and a shiny, sturdy new lock on the main door. I made it to the bottom stair and sunk onto it with a mixture of exhaustion, relief and exhilaration. I'd done it!! I'd really done it.

What now? I thought soberly. I couldn't believe there weren't a bunch of white-coated individuals coming after me. I looked again at the place I'd just left, and once more felt a flood of relief. I didn't know where I was or where I was going but at least I was no longer confined; I was totally spent.

Chapter Nineteen

I used the rickety railing that divided the front steps in half and climbed onto the porch. I found a corner that was concealed from the street and sidewalk by a half-wall that surrounded the porch on either side of the stairs. I prepared to lay down, rest, figure out what to do next but the smell of urine and shriek of nearby sirens made me hesitate. Then it dawned on me that when I was missed, police could be notified, the area surrounding the hospital would be searched, I'd be found.

I struggled to my feet; I needed direction, an objective, but first I had to try and clear my head and get far away from here. I needed to find out not only where I'd been but where I was going.

In the back of my mind I kept hearing, "Hilly, Hilly, Hilly," and at first I didn't understand the significance. Then it dawned on me, I'd get to Maine, the edge of the earth and find Hilly.

I started walking away from the hospital area, nearly a block away and through the run¬down neighborhood with its dilapidated buildings. I walked along the crack and weed-filled sidewalk hearing the sirens retreating in the distance, listening to the barking dogs and summer noises of a city unknown.

Soon, at the foot of a small hill, I saw a sign, 'Congress Street.' Without knowing why, I headed toward a statue of a large man sitting in a chair. With several streets intersecting there, it looked as though this was the center of something—just what, I had no idea, but I wouldn't find out standing here on the street corner. The statue was at least eight city blocks away, clearly visible, but still some distance from where I stood weak and wobbly. I headed toward my objective.

I passed a woman pushing a grocery cart with squeaky wheels along the sidewalk. The cart was filled to overflowing with plastic bags with thick plastic handles tethered to the top wire of the cart. These held brightly colored bits of clothing, scarves perhaps, and cheap beads or other synthetic baubles. One such bag held a lone child's doll, plump, dirty and naked with a joyous facial expression and matted golden ringlets—an obscene captive of the filthy old woman and her bag. The woman herself mumbled unintelligibly as I came close to her. She looked at me with fearful, darting eyes, streaks of dirt on her wrinkled face and garish red lipstick on and beyond her lips. Heavy rouge, like you don't see on anyone but the very old, caked her cheeks like an overdone Santa Claus working double shifts. Pieces of steel grey hair, chunked together with endless sweating and no bathing were escaping from the wool babushka she had wrapped around her head.

What an apparition—I'd never seen anything like this! As I passed her I noticed she had on at least two pairs of socks, all mismatched and the elasticity long gone. She had on a pair of polyester pants that came to her shins—whether by design or original or shrunken size who could tell? Over the pants she wore a dress and a skirt. A dingy white cardigan sweater completed the outfit, and although it was now August and quite warm, she had an oversized white 'great-coat' over her shoulders. A pair of hard plastic pop beads from the early sixties hung from around her neck along with a rotten Goody hairbrush.

"Hello," I said gently as I passed her. She did not respond; she did not smile back. She just kept pushing her pile of rubble to nowhere.

I shrugged, feeling very badly for this person who I thought had once been beautiful, probably with a normal life and goals. I felt now that I did not stand out as much as I feared. I also knew I did not have far to go before I became that woman—or worse.

I trudged on trying to get the image of that woman out of my mind. It was horrible to think people were doomed to live like this, to spend their final days alone, wandering about, pushing stolen or abandoned grocery carts. *God, what in Hell was happening to this world? What had caused the awful changes from the time I grew up until now?* I wandered on, lost in thought. My own troubles were far from my mind for the moment.

I walked right into someone and lost my balance. I fell onto the brick sidewalk with a thud. I hadn't quite realized what had happened and was figuring that out when I saw the extended hand. I reached for it, offering an apology for not watching where I was going.

"I'm sorry, so sorry...lot on my mind...not paying attention. I didn't mean...are you okay?" I stammered.

"The question is, miss, are you okay? You are the one

who was unceremoniously dumped on her derriere on the sidewalk, you know?"

"Yes, yes, fine," I went on but I was far from fine. I was exhausted, afraid and now starved. I felt very alone and very much like crying. All these feelings came on me suddenly with the touch of another human being, the offer of a hand up, the concern in the low, measured voice....

With effort, I held these fragile emotions in check. After all, regardless of what I didn't have, I still retained my pride—my strength born of the hard life of midwestern farmers. It was ingrained in me, and I hoped would always be there to call upon if necessary.

Once again on my feet, I looked at the man who I'd walked into. Actually not a lot different from the woman with the cart except that he had on fine clothes, a three-piece wool suit, dirty and frayed with over wearing but there was no question it had once been an expensive purchase. He wore a white shirt, buttoned to the neck, also frayed, but worn with pride. I felt this man had dignity and a life of success or privilege. What had happened to him? *How did people end up like this?* I asked for the second time that hour.

"Well then, if you're sure you are okay, I shall be off."

"I'm sorry," I apologized again.

"No harm done, miss," he called over his shoulder as he walked off.

"Wait, sir, mister. Could I ask you something, please?"

He turned, seemed to study me for a moment and returned to my side.

"Why certainly, miss. What is it you wish to know?"

He seemed so poised, so articulate, refined.

"Well, I, ah, I'm lost," I finally managed to say.

"Ah ha. Can you tell me where it is you wish to go?"

He stood very close to me now, studying me, possibly recognizing the 'skirt' of the trademark hospital johnnie. I caught the slightest hint of alcohol on his breath and looked at him in surprise.

I was obviously poor at disguising my discovery because he nodded to me, patted his inside jacket pocket where I could now see the outline of a flask or maybe a pint bottle. "My wife, alas, I am a slave to her will," he said as a statement of fact, not an apology.

"Oh, well, I like CC and Ginger myself," I offered for no particular reason.

"Gin," he said, once again patting his 'wife.'

"Now then, how can I be of assistance?"

"I, I have been through an ordeal—an accident, I guess you could say. I've lost my friends and everything I own but I know teachers in Portland, Maine, and I want to find them. I remember the address of one of them but not the street number." I caught my breath, amazed I'd been able to put all that together.

"Actually, I don't know how far I've come or how far I have to go because I don't know where I am now."

He had remained unreadable throughout my monologue but he raised his eyebrows at my last revelation.

For a second I felt uneasy. Had I revealed too much? Was this man capable of mugging? Murder? Would he turn me in to the officials?

Again, he seemed to read my mind.

"Rest easy, little one, I will not harm you."

I smiled up at him. I did not think he was older than I, but I felt better, safer for the term—little one—like I had a protector if only for the briefest period. I was not in this alone. And then he started to laugh a great, hearty laugh.

I took a step back. The man was crazy—what had I done?

He stopped laughing immediately. "I'm so sorry," he said. "It is just that your worries are totally unfounded. You see, you are in Portland, Maine!"

"Maine General Trauma Center that way," he pointed in the general direction I'd come. At the same time, he glanced again at me and the hospital johnnie hanging below the oversize white shirt I'd purloined from the very same hospital.

Well, I couldn't help thinking, *for a tippler, he doesn't seem to miss much.* And, he didn't appear at all impaired. He didn't even have the ruddy complexion of a drinker. And his teeth were white and straight.

"And way out, several miles probably, there's a large shopping plaza and some discount stores, fast food places and an entrance to the Maine Turnpike—north and south bound. So you see, you're not as bad off as you thought you were. At least you've arrived at your destination," he smiled evenly.

Boy, I marveled to myself, *he does dispense practical information. It's as though he understands what might be important to me.* I sensed that this was a very intelligent, rather amazing actually, probably very cultured individual. Qualities like his came across even though so cleverly disguised.

"And, this way," he continued, pointing toward the statue, "is Longfellow Square. The poet's actual house is a mile or so down this main street. There are small shops, an eatery or so, a 'school of beauty',"—he smiled as he said that—"and eventually, the waterfront. There are some soup kitchens, a Salvation Army office with its store, as well as homeless shelters in the vicinity also." I could only imagine what he thought looking at me. Doubtful he considered I was a runaway, since people in their forties don't run away. And then it was my turn to laugh. *Of course, they do!* I thought. I was a perfect example! I just hadn't run away in the usual teenage sense.

"Something I said?" he raised his eyebrows and adjusted his vest slightly to align perfectly.

"Oh, sorry, no. I was just imagining what a sight I must present."

"Ah," he said. "Don't give that a second thought. Long ago I learned not to judge a book by its cover. Please pardon the cliché here. Now take my wife for example." He gestured toward the direction of the hospital, where standing on a corner a few blocks away, stood the woman with the shopping cart.

"What," I gasped, "that woman is your wife?" I asked in disbelief. "Really?"

"Yes, really," he said and his face looked sad and years older than it had just minutes ago.

"Oh, I'm sorry, so sorry. I didn't mean...."

"Well, don't apologize. Life is a funny thing—you start out well, perhaps with everything, and a few misfortunes, illness," he paused, "well, it really doesn't take an earthquake or flood to turn everything upside down."

"My gosh, but...." Suddenly I'd forgotten my own feelings, problems.

"But well, what do you say we grab a bite to eat? There's a nice comfy café, run by Stefan, a Moroccan," he chuckled good naturedly, "on the next block. They have some very hearty beef stew and a decent American section on their menu, booths, and" he patted his other breast pocket, "you can still smoke there!"

"Oh, I'd love to," I answered honestly, "but what about your wife?"

"She'll be fine," he smiled. "She will follow me if I stop following her." I raised my eyes to his, confused with that last remark.

"It's a tad complicated but I will tell you about it if you are interested."

"Yes, very." I couldn't help myself; my mind was swimming. "But I have no money," I said, then added quickly, "with me."

"Well, I invited you to join me so naturally it is my treat," he beamed. And with that, this courtly gentleman glanced toward his wife, looped his arm through mine, lending support to his fine company.

When we were comfortably seated in a large corner booth overlooking the street, a smiling waitress appeared with huge white menus. She leaned across the table, produced a silver pitcher from somewhere behind her and started filling our water glasses.

"Be back shortly," she said. "Make yourself comfortable! Holler if you are ready to order before I return."

And with that and a slight wave, she was gone. She disappeared through a set of swinging double doors behind the counter.

I looked at the menu—it was gigantic in size and covered in heavy plastic. I could barely hold it upright. I flipped through several pages of Moroccan dishes, appetizers, sides and luncheon combinations. Despite my hunger, I really didn't care for the very spicy odors emanating from the kitchen.

Quickly I reviewed the American Cuisine, which really was quite expansive. "I'd like a cup of beef stew, if I may?"

"Oh no, my dear, you really must have more than that. Please let me order for you."

And for the first time in hours, I thought of Slade and longed to know what had happened to him, if I'd ever see him again and if I'd ever see Bish or Paddy. My head began to throb anew. Without even being conscious of my action, I reached to message my temples.

"Headache?"

"Yes, a little," I replied softly.

"Here," he said and reached into an inside coat pocket and withdrew a little tin of Bufferin. He tapped out two and handed them to me. His hands were immaculate—a fact that had escaped me when he helped me from the sidewalk.

I took the pills gratefully and washed them down with an entire glass of water. I was very thirsty, too, I realized.

"Okay, then, here we go", he took a deep breath as the waitress approached and stood by the table, poised with pen and pad in hand.

He ordered a virtual feast: "Steak-medium, squash-side, mashed potatoes, gravy, peas, applesauce, rolls and butter, of course."

The waitress wrote hurriedly, stopped and smiled at my benefactor.

He smiled back graciously, then added, "For two, oh, and a cup of your best beef stew and two slices of apple pie for dessert and a cup of black coffee, please."

"Stew first?" she asked.

"Yes, and the coffee and milk, rolls and butter, too, please."

"Yes, sir. Thank you, Sir Walter."

I was astounded at the size and scope of the order and didn't even try to hide my surprise. I never would have presumed to order that much food but it was everything I loved—basic food—meat and potatoes. Again I had this strange sensation, it was as though he knew me, could read my thoughts.

I got the impression that the 'Sir' was for real. I thought how extraordinary it was to meet this man. I couldn't wait to hear his story. Everything seemed so bizarre, yet he seemed secure and composed in what I could only imagine was far from his normal environment.

"All that food," was all I could manage to get out.

"Don't worry," he winked at me, "I can afford it."

I looked at his earnest, patrician face.

"Really," he added.

"Walter Parks-Hyde at your service," he said, formally.

"Pleased to meet you, Sir Walter, I'm Evie."

The waitress returned with the first round of our repast.

"Oh, I really should wash my hands. May I be excused, Sir Walter?"

"Of course, Evie."

"Right to the back on your left," the waitress supplied.

"Thank you," I said and slid to the corner of the booth and out.

After I washed my hands and did the best I could to clean some of the grime off my face with paper towels, I returned…to an empty booth!

I whipped my head around to search for Sir Walter.

"Outside with his wife. He said to go ahead and start and he'd be back shortly," said the waitress reassuringly. "C'mon, dig in while it's hot," she encouraged.

I needed no more encouragement. I slid back into the booth, buttered a roll, ate a spoonful of the delicious stew, took a sip of milk and a bite of the warm roll and as discreetly as I could, I turned slightly to look out the large plate glass window behind me.

I could see them across the street huddled together in the recess of an old, large brick building. I couldn't help noticing that the architecture of this area was extraordinary! Satisfied that I hadn't lost Sir Walter and that his wife had indeed followed him, I concentrated on eating.

As I finished my last spoonful of stew, the rest of the meal arrived and with that, so did Sir Walter with his wife in tow. I glanced across the street to where they'd been but there was no shopping cart in the doorway, nor could I see it on the sidewalk or anywhere else from my vantage point. I shrugged my shoulders and turned my attention to Sir Walter and his wife.

"Elizabeth, this is my new friend, Evie, and Evie, I would like to present my wife, Elizabeth."

"I'm pleased to meet you, ma'am," I said sliding along the booth to rise at the introduction. I nodded my head and added a slight curtsy, though I did not know exactly why I did. I just felt like I should use my best manners. I returned to my seat.

"Elizabeth does not like to feel penned up," he explained as she fairly perched on the outside corner of the booth cushion.

Sir Walter slid in next to me in the seat he'd occupied before he'd gone to fetch his wife. She sat opposite him on her perch.

"Excuse me, Rose, a bowl of your famous beef stew for our Elizabeth, here, if you please."

"Certainly, Sir," she replied and immediately disappeared behind the swinging doors. She returned a minute later with the steaming bowl of stew on her upheld tray.

147

We all ate heartily. Most conversation ceased during the meal but I glanced at them from time-to-time as I ate.

I was surprised and pleased to see that Elizabeth had decided to join us. I felt a little guilty for borrowing her husband when she so obviously needed him—or did she? I was a bit disappointed because I wanted to hear Sir Walter's story. I knew it had to be fascinating and he was unlikely to relate it now that his wife was here.

"How is everything?"

"Fine, Rose, fine."

I smiled in agreement with Sir Walter's assessment. He smiled back at me then looked at Elizabeth, busy with her stew, and nodded to Rose.

Elizabeth said nothing; she never looked up from her stew. Sir Walter placed a pat of butter and a roll on a small plate by his wife's bowl of stew. She ate slowly, deliberately, with the impeccable manners of the well born and bred.

"May I be excused now?" she asked in a small, childlike voice and for the first time raised her eyes to look directly at Sir Walter.

"Certainly, my dear." He attempted to stand from his place in the booth.

Without another word, she slid from her perch and walked to the back of the restaurant. Sir Walter sat back down but watched the door his wife had entered. Several minutes passed and just as I thought I detected some concern in Sir Walter's expression, the door opened and Elizabeth emerged.

With her eyes fastened firmly on the floor looking neither right nor left, she walked directly to the front of the restaurant and directly out the door to the sidewalk. Sir Walter excused himself immediately and was outside by her side in a second.

Arm-in-arm, he escorted her back across the street and back to the doorway where I'd last seen her with her cart. She sat on the stone steps and bowed her head. As I watched her, Sir Walter appeared from the side pushing her cart. I hadn't even realized he'd stepped away from her momentarily. I watched as he bent down to her and wondered what he was doing or saying. I couldn't tell from my vantage point at the window. For a moment, I wondered if he'd return to the restaurant or stay with Elizabeth.

Almost before I could finish my thought, he was back in the booth.

"Is there some other dessert you'd care for?" Sir Walter asked. "You don't have to eat the apple pie if you'd prefer something else. I should have asked about that, really. You know they have a wonderful bread pudding here and they make their whip cream from scratch. It's Elizabeth's favorite, actually."

"Ah, no thank you though. I can't eat another bite— of anything. I am wonderfully full. I can't believe I ate so much as it is. Thank you so much for bringing me here and for this excellent meal. I'm grateful for your company and kindness," I added quickly. I was suddenly a little nervous and uncomfortable and the words began to pour out.

"Yes, yes, you are entirely welcome," Sir Walter said as he patted my hand reassuringly. Obviously, the gentleman in him sensed my awkwardness and wanted to put me at ease.

"Really, this was my pleasure," and the sincerity in his voice was unmistakable.

"Your wife, Elizabeth, how...," I started to ask how they'd met then thought I should not.

He hesitated for what seemed like the longest time and

when I looked at him to see his expression, I caught him staring at the metal and flesh forms in the doorway across the street.

"Yes, Elizabeth," he said finally, slowly. "We've come far—she and I. Been together for a long time, travelled a long way to this door step." He half-nodded toward Elizabeth.

I wanted to tell him he didn't have to share this private history with me, but I could not because I was mesmerized by his look, his voice, his story. He was very self-contained but there was a passion, an urgency to him. I wanted to hear what he had to say—more than that—I felt he needed to say it. I was transfixed.

"Elizabeth and I are very distant cousins, minor royals, born and raised in England on old, rambling neighboring estates in the country. Elizabeth is older than I by seven years but from the time I saw her at age four or five, I believe I knew she would always be in my life.

"During my school years, Eton and Oxford, of course— it was the family tradition, and in those days one did what was expected. Generations of my family preceded me and I was destined to follow in their well-heeled footsteps until one day when I would take possession of the family's land and estates. But I always loved Elizabeth more than any other thing and she was the only thing I wanted to possess, if you'll pardon my expression. And she envisioned and wanted a different life than the one that was in store for me.

"She went to boarding school in the United States, travelled a great deal, and was much admired and sought after for her great beauty, witty conversation and independent streak. But I had spoken for her early and years later, she confessed to me that she had always known that it would be me whom she would wed.

"At first, we were deliriously happy. We'd been married in the traditional lavish wedding befitting our station in life. We skied, sunned, visited our many friends the world over and I was thoroughly satisfied and ready to return to our home, start our family and live the life of the landed gentry, as was now expected of us. There were only two problems.

Elizabeth did not want to live in the country; she did not want a family. I should have been devastated but she had become my raison d'etre—my reason for being, as it were...." He paused and looked at me.

"Can you imagine?" he asked and I nodded. Oh, yes, I could imagine, I thought.

"She still is," he added as if it were necessary. I felt the well of tears at the back of my eyes as I imagined his situation and his love for her. No one had ever loved me like that. I wondered for a moment how many women had ever known that depth of love. Until now and Elizabeth Barrett Browning notwithstanding, I hadn't even contemplated that a person could love to that degree selflessly and, apparently, endlessly. Especially today—people often dropped each other at the first sign of illness or insanity.

I was trying to define the extraordinary lengths he'd gone to and continued to go to just to keep her—*or the shell of her,* I thought with sadness, in his life.

He cleared his throat just then and continued.

"I made certain, ah," he paused and looked toward the ceiling as he sought the right word to use next, "ah, arrangements which enabled the family estate and holdings to remain intact and so on, and Elizabeth and I began our journey together in earnest.

"We climbed the highest peaks, toasted fabulous sunsets, watched shooting stars, sailed the most dangerous

151

oceans—just the two of us. We ate exotic foods, slept in the highest and lowest accommodations all over the world, we loved and lived as few are privileged to do, and lucky—lucky because we had found one another early, known one another only, loved one another totally and we lived through our high adventures and misadventures," he chuckled at that, then went on, "and through it all, 'we two were one.'"

I swiped at the corner of my eye hoping he did not see the wetness there, but he was in another place reliving his bliss, possibly for the last time, the greatest love he knew.

How I envied Elizabeth, the love of her life, the love of this man, the strength and independence to live her life as she chose, the good fortune that the love of her life would abandon everything to follow her—just to be with her. My breath caught in my throat as I realized the implications. Tears stung my eyes; I wiped them and looked at Sir Walter.

He was staring at me intently.

"It's... it's just so...beautiful," I managed to whisper.

"Yes," he said simply.

"A few years ago, Elizabeth began to change in the smallest of ways. She talked of starting a family for the first time since we married. By the by, Elizabeth is seventy-seven now," he said and stared pointedly at me.

I said nothing but glanced out the window to where she still sat on the steps across the street. I could guess where this was going.

"Yes," he nodded as he spoke. He could follow my eyes and read my thoughts. "Well, mercifully it was slow and in the beginning she submitted to my dragging her to the finest doctors, clinics, alternative spas and health centers in the world.

"Finally, we came to America, away from our families.

We didn't want our people to see us like this. There was nothing we tried that could change the course of things; it was a relatively slow process and we adjusted as best we could. I got a nice place on the Western Prom but we're never there. Elizabeth wandered off more and more, developed odd habits, began to inhabit a world she could not share with me...

He sighed. "Now, sometimes she wanders for days on end—round- and-round. Occasionally, I will get a room whenever and wherever I can convince her to stop for a bit. We wash, eat and then we leave." He sighed then continued.

"Occasionally Elizabeth will pick trash, sort through cans, talk to pigeons but not people. For the most part, I'm grateful she lets me follow her—responds to me at all. I can't stop her and I can't help her so I follow her and I have a nip here and there to keep me company." He patted his pocket flask. His face flushed with embarrassment. "But I will be here when she needs me and I keep hoping that one day she won't wander and I won't nip anymore."

I looked at him and he smiled faintly. I could see that he had lost all hope for that day though he said otherwise.

"Every day they make progress, come out with new drugs, find treatments and cures for the most impossible diseases," I tried to encourage him.

"Yes," he agreed, "but nothing that reverses the demon...." he said as his voice trailed off.

We sat there for some time, each with our own thoughts. I envied his memories. They'd lived their lives, experienced life on high and even now continued to live as circumstances allowed. Possibly he'd lost hope that they could cure Elizabeth but he had definitely not given up. He was still there by her side—his beloved Elizabeth. I could see that the two were still one.

"So let me take care of this," he patted the slip the waitress had discreetly left. "Then we will see if we can find your friend. How will that be?"

"Yes, fine," I said softly. "Thank you so very much. Thank you for everything!"

I couldn't help myself. I had to add, "You know you've lived a love story—your love is so inspiring. I wish I could write because I would like to share this with others—to let them know love like this—true and pure and everlasting... actually exists. I...I just, ah, I'd...."

"I know," he said softly, "Thank you." And with that, he excused himself, slid out of the booth and took the bill to the register.

I sat quietly lost in thought, overwhelmed by this gentleman and his capacity to live and love and cope so graciously with the cruel hand life had dealt his dear Elizabeth. For a moment, I forgot my aches and pains, woes, and even what I was doing here.

I couldn't help but wonder how Elizabeth would have described their life together—their love—if she'd been able. But even though the story had been related simply by Sir Walter, it had been delivered eloquently. The summary had all the poignancy of a thousand pages of *The Greatest Love on Earth.* The fact that it was shared by a man for probably the first time in his life was not lost on me. I felt privileged, indeed; I would have traded my life for the one Elizabeth lived, even now, I thought as I stared across the street at her with her cart.

I was aware of a movement to my left and quickly turned to see Sir Walter as he slid back into the booth in one fluid motion. He was still a handsome man, I realized. Tan, lithe, and agile even now. His manner seemed to imply that all this had not taken much of a toll on him and I guessed it must be so.

Maybe it was genetic, I found myself wondering. He certainly had the means to live otherwise but not the will to force anything unwanted on his beloved. I wondered where they slept when Elizabeth was in her wandering mode....

"Ah, here we are then. I have secured a current phone book for the Greater Portland Area and been assured that it will also have the harbor and its islands. We shall see if we can find your friend's number and give her a call. Shall we?

"Now, what did you say your friend's name is?" Sir Walter asked.

"It's Hilly, ah Hildegard...." I paused as I realized I couldn't remember her last name. Embarrassed, I looked at Sir Walter as if he could help me. He smiled patiently.

"Oh," I blushed as it came to me. "Hildegarde Martin on Sterling's Island." The words tumbled out as I remembered the words written on the paper Hilly gave me in Nassau.

"Good, good," Sir Walter said as he began flipping through the phone book.

"Ah, here we are, I think. H. Martin, 11 Elm Street, Sterling's Island." He slipped a small elegant leather notebook from an inside pocket and pulled a clean piece of paper from it. I could see his gold leaf monogram on the cover as he held it in one hand while writing with the other. I couldn't help but marvel at his fine script as he jotted down the information for me. His hand was strong and steady and I realized that I hadn't seen him take a nip for some time now.

Had he been preoccupied or did he not really drink that much, after all? I asked myself. I took that paper he held out to me. There was change between his fingers and he placed that in the palm of my other hand.

"The phone is in the back by the ladies room," he supplied helpfully. He smiled at me. Immediately, I got up to place the call and he slid out to let me pass. I was instantly aware of my circumstances and how I looked. Sir Walter had not asked any questions but I felt compelled to tell him a little about myself before we parted company. I thought I owed him at least that much after all he'd done for me. I never got the chance.

Hilly had answered my call on the first ring. Of all things, she was expecting a call from Mary and Bill who, she told me excitedly, should be arriving in Portland any time now.

Fate, I wondered as Hilly rattled off instructions. She asked me where I was and told me she'd send a cab directly to the restaurant to collect me and my things. "The cab," she explained "will pick you up in front and take you directly to the ticket office at the ferry terminal. Wait in the terminal and you can come across with Mary and Bill. I'll tell them you are there when they call—but you may run into them first. Oh, they'll be so happy," she almost shouted, and then she hung up before I could say another word.

"Oh my Lord," I groaned, my head suddenly pounding again.

"Here," I turned as I heard Sir Walter's now-familiar voice.

I turned around and he stood there with a bottle of aspirin in one out-stretched hand and a bundle of clothing clutched to his chest with the other. "Take these," he shook the pills out of the bottle into my palm, "Two now and two in four to six hours and—try these things on and see if anything fits." He passed the items to me. I could only imagine he'd gotten these from Elizabeth's cart when he'd sent me to the phone.

I was too grateful and touched by his thoughtfulness to wonder too much about the clothing's origins.

I slipped inside, put the two aspirin in my mouth, washed them down with a handful of water from the tap. I spread the things from the bundle onto the counter beside the sink. I was surprised to see that these clothes were clean and in very good shape; they were also quality pieces— designer labels, no less.

I quickly slipped into a pair of white short-shorts, which I used as underwear, and pulled on a light silk sleeveless dress. Then I put on the white shirt I'd stolen from the hospital. I didn't button it but pulled the sides together at the bottom and tied a knot. I looked down at my feet—the ankle length hospital "slippers" and dirty white sneakers.

I laughed aloud as I studied myself in the mirror on the far wall. *What a sight!* But I was darned glad for the change of clothes. I threw the johnnies and the bathrobe into the waste can, washed up in the sink and covered the laundry with used paper towels.

I felt much better as I emerged from the ladies room. *How long has it been since I've worn real clothes?* I wondered.

"Oh good, good—you look fine," said Sir Walter as he took my arm and escorted me toward the front of the restaurant.

"Your cab is here, my dear Evie," he said and smiled brightly when he saw the wonder on my face. "Cab driver came in and asked for Evie—his fare to the waterfront," he explained.

"Oh," I managed.

"Why have you done all this for me? How can I ever thank you enough, Sir Walter."

"My dear, you already have. It was a pleasure spending

time with you this afternoon. You know," he said and paused, "you remind me very much of Elizabeth—ah Elizabeth when she was young." And then I understood.

"Good luck to you, Evie," he said as he opened the cab door and pressed some bills into my hand.

He closed the door, patted the roof of the cab a couple of times and we pulled away. The last time I saw him, he was waving goodbye as he made his way across the street back to his precious Elizabeth.

I waved to him, too. I glanced at my hand still clutching the bills Sir Walter had given me—two twenties and a fifty. Tears filled my eyes and I had a lump in my throat that I just couldn't swallow.

CHAPTER TWENTY

The ferry terminal was not much more than a mile from the restaurant and was a beehive of activity! There were people in every type of outfit so I shouldn't stand out too much, I thought. I was a little self-conscious, I realized. I glanced around as I waited for the cab driver to make change for me.

He gave me my change and I stepped from the cab onto the sidewalk beside the building. There were benches all around the good-sized building and people hurrying this way and that. I saw some candy and soda machines, lockers and sign boards with everything from real estate ads to a ménage of business cards tacked this way and that. One board held a sample of T-shirts, sweatshirts and caps with the ferry's name and logo on the items. I was tempted to buy a sweatshirt but didn't know how much it was or how much the boat ticket would cost. I also didn't know how long this gift from Sir Walter would have to last. I didn't know if I'd ever get my things back—my brooch and my money and...would I get a job somewhere or what? Everything was so up-in-the-air and I didn't have a clue. As

I started to think about my predicament, my future, my head began to pound again and I knew I'd better take things one step-at-a-time or I'd drive myself crazy.

This was all too much, I thought.

I saw a sign that read, 'TICKETS,' and two windows near the front of the room and automatically made my way to the shorter line.

"Can I help you?" came the cheery request.

"Sterling's Island, please."

"Three dollars round-trip."

I slid the money under the window and waited for her to make change. Then I asked her where I should go to get the boat.

She gave me the ticket and my change and pointed, saying, "Gate 5, ma'am, right out there."

I followed where her finger pointed with my eyes and saw the brightly painted boats lining the dock. I pushed open one of the heavy glass doors and headed in the direction she'd pointed. I was trying to stay upright in the moving crowd while jockeying for position when I heard the familiar voice of Bill Tanner.

"Hey, we've been looking for you!" I felt Bill's hand on my shoulder and turned to greet him.

Not seeing Mary, I asked, "Oh, Bill, am I ever glad to see you! Where's Mary? I thought she was going to be with you."

"She's inside getting the tickets—it's her turn this year." He smiled as he looked at me. "You look great—really, really great," Bill whispered as he appraised me approvingly. I could feel my face redden. "I, I'm sure I look a fright, Bill. You're just trying to be nice to me since you haven't seen me for a while." I was embarrassed and tried to distract him.

"You wouldn't believe the week I've had," I added lamely.

"Hey there you—you old devil, you," Mary chimed in. Beaming, she stepped forward and gave a big enough hug to take my breath away!

"It's so wonderful to see you again, Evie! We were wondering if you'd make it for the reunion. Oh, I'm just so glad you did and so is Bill," she added glancing at Bill.

"All aboard for Sterling's Island. Now boarding at Gate Five for Sterling's Island. All Aboard!" The announcement interrupted Mary so she shrugged her shoulders and gave a helpless look at the loudspeaker on the dock. She stepped away from me.

I almost dropped to the wharf. I hadn't realized that she was just about supporting me. I guessed I was in worse shape than I thought.

"We'll catch up on the boat ride and when we get to Hilly's," she promised when the announcement ended.

As I shuffled forward toward the loading ramp, I was suddenly self-conscious. I noticed all the people and their various attire. I was surprised but quite relieved to see that I didn't look all that out-of-place, except that I more resembled the younger generation wearing all types of dirty, ill-fitting or baggy clothes with unlaced or half-laced sneakers.

I heard someone yell, "Tickets, please," but I couldn't see them through all the boarders.

"Oh, ah, here you are," I said as I soon passed the young man holding his hand out for my ticket.

I made my way across the metal plank and onto the boat. I stood off to one side and waited for Bill and Mary. I watched as they came across the metal span single file.

"My goodness, you sure have a lot of stuff," I heard myself saying when Mary was aboard. "Are you going right to school from Hilly's?" I asked.

"Oh, Lord, no," I heard Mary answer as she stashed her many Bean bags, knapsack, and other canvas totes by the smokestack. "We always bring plenty...never know when you're gonna need an extra sweatshirt or—heaven forbid—a jacket! These Maine nights, even in the summer, can get plenty cold when you're on the water."

"We're here for two weeks anyway, so we come prepared," Bill chimed in. "Evie, where are your bags? You didn't leave them in the waiting room, did you?" he teased.

I started to reply but there was an announcement coming over the loud speaker. "Long story. I'll tell you later," I added quickly and smiled at Bill. It was so nice to see a familiar face.

We found seats and I tried to relax while the Captain or crew member explained, "Cover your ears when the loud horn blows," and that there was no smoking anywhere on the vessel....

I leaned my head back and closed my eyes, exhausted now that I was in relative safety. I must have been moving on pure adrenalin and now I was feeling achy, weak and a little light-headed.

The boat backed out of its slip and was soon in Portland Harbor heading to Sterling's Island and Hilly. I noticed an immediate drop in temperature once we were out of the inner harbor. The crisp breeze was quite invigorating and made me feel a lot better. I kept my eyes closed, head tilted back and drank in the smell of salt air, the cries of the seagulls flying overhead and Bill's soothing voice as he pointed out the various lighthouses and forts of Casco Bay.

Oh, this was just heavenly, I thought.

Even with all the action overhead and Bill's narration,

I could hear the buzz of conversation in the background but I didn't let it disturb my reverie. The sounds and smells and gentle sea breeze had me in their thrall and seemed like just the therapy I needed.

"God, I just love this!" I heard Bill exclaim with more emotion than I thought him capable of.... Generally, he was a fairly quiet, studious gentleman, although he had an excellent sense of humor and he did know how to have a good time—at least I thought I remembered he did. It was hard to believe that I'd known Bill and Mary for such a short time. They'd greeted me like a long lost friend and seemed genuinely delighted that I was going to Hilly's with them.

I was very glad to be with them but once again I was reminded of the *Victoria E.* and the three friends I'd left aboard. The time I'd spend with Paddy, Bish and Slade was beginning to seem like a dream, almost surreal. I determined that I would rest and get my strength back at Hilly's and as soon as possible, I'd make inquiries to the Caribbean authorities. I would find Paddy, Bish and Slade or I would find out what had happened to them. I'd also like to find out what had happened to me... For a moment, I thought wistfully of my brooch, which was far more important to me than my money and other possessions but in the scheme of things, it was my friends and their wellbeing that mattered most.

I felt a bump and was aware that people were gathering their stuff and getting ready to disembark the passenger ferry. Another jarring sensation and the screech of wood and metal rubbing together and I reluctantly opened my eyes. As I did, someone fell against me.

"Oh, I'm so sorry. I wasn't paying attention. Lost my balance there."

"Uh, umm," I muttered as the pain screeched through my head and my foot hurt because someone was standing on it. The weight suddenly lifted.

"Oh, Evie, are you all right?" Bill and Mary asked in unison.

"Yes, just fine. I'm fine, really. Thank you," I managed and smiled convincingly, I hoped.

"Here, let me help you up." I felt a strong arm under my elbow gently lifting me to my feet.

"My name is Micah," the well-muscled young man offered.

I looked him full in the face. This face was regularly kissed by the summer sun. His red hair was thick and well cut and he had boots on—white rubber boots that came to the knees of his well-washed, faded blue jeans. He wore a short-sleeve shirt with a purple racing stripe across the chest.

"Hi, I'm Evie. You didn't hurt me, really," I lied.

"Oh, that wasn't me. I was standing next to the fellow when he fell on you. I'd be a pretty poor lobsterman if I couldn't keep my balance on a boat, don't you think?" and he laughed a hearty, wonderful laugh.

"Evie, c'mon," Mary was pulling my arm. "Look, there's Hilly, there on the dock. Evie, look—you're not looking, Evie!"

I tore my eyes away from Micah the handsome lobsterman and looked to where Mary was pointing. Sure enough, there was dear Hilly waiting patiently on the edge of the wharf. We all waved a greeting as we proceeded to the gang plank.

"Hey, Mary, let me help you with this bag," I said and reached for the tote.

"Oh, Evie," she said, letting go of the bag. "I really

shouldn't have packed so much," she admitted sheepishly. "I do this every year and swear I'll travel lighter in the future. Somehow, I get worse every year, if anything," she laughed gaily.

For a moment we were enveloped in a mass of confusion. People meeting or greeting, people trying to locate kids or freight, others waiting to board the boat for the return trip to the city. It was utter chaos—downright crazy on this wharf. I kept my head down and tried to follow Mary's back in the general direction I'd seen Hilly standing.

Suddenly Hilly was hugging me and saying something I couldn't make out above the din of the crowd.

"What?" I mouthed.

"Oh, Evie, I'm just so glad you came. This is wonderful, wonderful, don't you think?" Hilly's enthusiasm was infectious.

"Oh yes, I do," I agreed.

CHAPTER TWENTY-ONE

There was a short blast of the horn and within a minute the swarm of people had vanished like locusts after devouring a crop.

We stood on the dock alone except for a small brown dog with no collar. The boat was on its way back to the mainland. The taxi and last of the arrivals were at the top of the hill, nearly out of sight.

"Well, what are you waiting for?" Hilly said, picking up a couple of the bags. "I hope you're all hungry," she said as she started up the wharf toward the cobblestone street.

"Oh, yes, starved," Mary said.

"I could eat something," Bill responded.

"Good, I started the grill before I came to pick you up. Should be ready by the time we get home. Got burgers and dogs, slaw, potato salad—you know, the BBQ works."

"Okay, gang, this is it." Hilly was busy putting luggage in the back of an ancient station wagon with wooden paneling.

"All aboard," she added gaily as she sprang into the driver's seat and got settled. "Everybody in?" she called over her shoulder as she started the engine, which purred away happily. "All set?"

"Ready."

"Yep, let's go, then," came the responses from her passengers.

"Okay, then," she said and put on her blinker as she looked over her shoulder and pulled a u-turn. We were now heading in the opposite direction of the way she was parked.

"I'll take you on a deluxe tour later if you don't mind. Right now, let's get home and eat. I'm famished!"

"Great!" Mary exclaimed, more or less echoing our feelings. I just didn't have the energy to take a tour right now but I was looking forward to getting to Hilly's and finding a comfortable spot to rest.

"I'll point out a few things on the way for you, Evie. You guys try not to be too bored," she said to Bill and Mary, who had gotten in the back seat and were beaming at each other.

I was sitting in the front seat and did my best to pay attention as Hilly dutifully pointed out several shops, the local grocery store, a B & B, the library, and fire station. Every now and then, we'd pass a car heading in the opposite direction and Hilly would wave or toot the horn lightly in response to their waves.

After a few minutes, we stopped at an intersection to let a car pass. There was no set of lights or stop signs, just a crossing of two roads.

"We're quite informal, as you can see," Hilly said as the person signaled and drove in front of us toward the ocean. I watched the car drive to a beautiful old building with lush, green grounds. I saw several tennis courts with sparkling blue water in the background.

"Oh, what a spot," I almost whispered—in awe at the sheer elegance of the entryway, the surrounding porch, latticework and colorful flowers in and around the building. For a moment, I thought of my friends and the beautiful building on the Caribbean Island where we'd shared our last meal.

"Oh, yes, I practically lived there as a young girl."

My attention returned to Hilly who was talking.

"It's the equivalent of a local yacht club," Hilly concluded. Then added, "That's where I learned to sail and play tennis and ping pong. Actually, I learned how to dance there, too!" she laughed unexpectedly as she remembered her youthful experiences. "It's where I had my first dance with a boy!" she added.

"We usually manage to get in some tennis while we're here—as Hilly's guests," Bill informed me from the back seat.

"Ah," I said, trying to sound enthusiastic. But I didn't play tennis that well and therefore wasn't all that fond of it. Now sailing, I thought, that might be fun. It had been years—a lifetime already—since I'd been sailing on the Charles River, but my recent experience had proven I did love the sport. I started to think of my brief time of two years in the east, of my one-time love, of....

"Okay, guys, we're almost home, Evie."

I was startled out of my reverie. I hadn't realized the car had stopped but Bill and Mary were already hauling the bags out of the back of the wagon.

"Here, let me help you," I said, making my way toward them.

"All set, let's go," said Hilly, who'd managed to throw a knapsack and pocketbook over her shoulders and was now leading us along a path that ran right beside the ocean. Further back, houses with lovely gardens and luxurious lawns sparsely dotted the landscape.

"Oh my," I exclaimed as a gust of salt air assailed me, titillating my senses.

"Neat, huh?" Mary giggled.

"Neat," I agreed and for a moment I forgot my exhaustion, pain, feelings of loss.

"This is it, Evie."

"Oh, my Lord, it's a mansion!" I couldn't help exclaiming.

"Not quite," Hilly laughed gaily. "Old family cottage— 'Grey Boulders'." She called back over her shoulder as she virtually ran up the dozen or so steps to the landing and then on to the next dozen until she skipped up the last few to the large deck.

By the time I got to the deck, my legs were shaking, my hands trembling and my head splitting. Still, I was impressed with the carrier-size deck. There was a grill, lounge chairs, regular deck chairs, various sundry patio furniture all tastefully arranged. Huge flower arrangements filled various standing wicker vases.

"Yes," Mary exclaimed enthusiastically, catching everyone off guard and making us laugh as she launched herself into the air and landed—luggage and all—on a heavily-cushioned, white wicker chaise lounge.

"Oh, she always does that when she arrives," said Bill by way of explanation. "One year she did it in the rain and I guess it's a tradition now—it is literally the first thing she does every time she gets here for vacation.

"Can you believe that?" he asked incredulously.

"Oh yes, I think I can," I answered as I sank into the

chaise next to Mary's. "Seems like an excellent tradition to me...."

"Okay, now who wants what?" Hilly asked.

"I'll have a burger with cheese on it if you have it." Mary ordered first.

"Of course I have it—it's called a cheeseburger here though," Hilly said in mock disdain. "And a hot dog, too, Mary?" Hilly asked.

"Yes, please," Mary answered somewhat embarrassed.

"And I'll have a couple cheeseburgers, well done, please." Bill requested, and added, "I'll take the bags up and make myself useful, okay?"

"Okay, the usual rooms then. Thanks, Bill." Hilly replied as she disappeared around the corner.

A moment later she returned with a tray full of goodies: a package of red hotdogs, a deli package of White American cheese, various mustards and relishes, chips, plate of hamburgers, a dish of pickles, a dish of sliced tomato, diced onions, and other items we couldn't see from our vantage point. We watched in awe as she set each thing onto one of the large wicker tables next to the grill.

"Now, what can I interest you in, Evie?" Hilly asked me.

"I'd love a red hotdog, please, Hilly!"

"And..."

"No *and*...I just ate before catching the boat to the island."

"Well, I know you told me that on the phone but you have no idea what this salt air can do to a normal appetite!"

"Ah, that's just what I need, a bigger appetite!"

Everyone laughed.

"Can I do anything?" Mary asked.

"Me, too," I chimed in.

"Oh, no, I'm all set, guys. You rest and relax for now. I'll holler if I need you."

"Okay, thanks," Mary and I said in unison.

"Eve, I'll show you your room, get you settled after lunch. You look pretty relaxed right now though."

We had sun tea with lunch, which was delicious. I even split a cheeseburger with Hilly. She'd brought sweet and dill pickles in addition to all the other vegetables and condiments. And she had homemade pickle relish from an old family recipe which I could have eaten out of the jar without any accompaniments.

We all complained that we'd eaten way too much and felt like pigs, but we were so utterly satiated that no one moved.

Bill, Mary, and Hilly sat around making small talk while I relaxed and listened to these old friends making plans, asking questions, and enjoying each other's company as they had every summer for years.

What a nice tradition, I thought as I drifted off to sleep with the sun's rays warming my hospital-white body.

CHAPTER TWENTY-TWO

I barely remember Hilly waking me and taking me to a guest room upstairs.

I mumbled thanks and climbed fully clothed into the most comfortable bed I'd ever slept in.

For the next day and a half, I slept. I have vague recollections of someone tipping a cup of tea to my lips and once I sat up and drank beef broth that Hilly brought me. At some point, I'd slipped out of my clothes and into an old chenille robe. There was just enough of a gentle breeze laden with salt and floral scents that cooled and soothed me. Hilly kept the old-fashioned dark green shades drawn all the way to the sill in the three front windows and three-quarters of the way down on the window beside where I lay. I thought I was in a very pleasant place somewhere between earth and heaven—a way-station. I was semi-aware yet seemingly in another world, or at least in another dimension.

In this state of mind, I thought about the time I spent in the East as a young girl; I thought of the first man I loved and I wondered what might have been had he returned and come for me in Ohio. I thought of my parents, gentle and strong—the people whose love for one another had brought me into the world. My parents, perhaps the people I most adored and admired—my only experience with unconditional love. Now I wondered why I never finished college. *Was it because I was brokenhearted when I lost my love to the war in a foreign land or was it because I was so homesick for my family?* Why was I asking these questions, having such thoughts at this time?

Crazy, crazy, was I losing my mind? I wondered.

Then it dawned on me. I was dying. At first, the thought bothered me—more than bothered me, it devastated me. I had done nothing with my life and it was my fault. My parents never held me back. They were quiet, solid, supportive in everything I thought I wanted to do. I realized now that it was me who thought of goals then never followed through. I was an empty vessel, a failure—my very own creation with only myself to blame if I died now.

Just for a second I thought about my physical state, the pain in my head. Was I bleeding somewhere in the skull? But I hadn't taken aspirin in over twenty-four hours and my head didn't really feel that bad now.

Anyway, I wasn't done yet. I couldn't die now. I wouldn't! I had to find out what happened in the Caribbean. I had to know about Paddy, Bish and Slade. This was one thing I would finish if it was the last thing I did.

I got out of bed fully alive and aware for the first time in how long? I didn't know how long, but I did have a purpose. I looked around the room.

I saw the bath and face towels and wash cloth neatly folded on the oak bureau near the door. I also found a set of underwear and clothes arranged carefully beside a toothbrush, Goody comb & brush set, shampoo and razor with gel.

Hmmm, shorts and T-shirt...perfect I thought and went across the hall to the upstairs bathroom. Halfway there, I heard laughter coming from the open window at the opposite end of the long hallway. "Ah, they're here sunning on the porch," I said to myself and couldn't wait to join them. I felt I was among friends and I was happy and grateful at the same time.

Chapter Twenty-Three

I took a luxurious bath, shampooed my hair and shaved my legs then a quick shower to rinse shampoo and soap from my head and body. I pulled the large bath towel around me and shook my head, combing my hair with my spread fingers. I rinsed the tub and moisturized my arms and legs, brushed my teeth twice. Suddenly alive and caring about every sensation, I carefully pulled on underwear, white shorts, T-shirt, and slipped on the rubber thongs I'd found inside the pile of clothing.

It's true, I thought. *Cleanliness is next to Godliness*—like I was the first to discover this fact. I felt like a new woman! I put my hand on the railing and walked along the top of the staircase. I wanted to jump for joy I felt so good but I knew I'd probably trip on the flip-flops and fall down the stairs and break my neck. I didn't need that. Maybe when I'd mastered walking in the rubber feet things I'd be more adventurous.

Carefully, I made my way down the stairs; slap, slap, slap went the things on my feet but I was grateful for them and the clothes. Hilly, I imagined, was the thoughtful provider... what a hostess! I was starving but resisted going through the kitchen. Instead, I took a left at the bottom of the stairs in front of a huge brick fireplace surrounded by books. I made a mental note to peruse the titles sometime. I loved books! I also saw all the items on the mantel and the arresting artwork in gilded frames carefully hung on the wall behind the large, comfortable-looking sofa. I padded over the rich green carpet with impossibly thick pile and took in all the perfectly matched furniture and drapes. The drapes and the sofa and many throw pillows were of the same material and had obviously been custom made for someone of exquisite taste.

Finally, I opened the screen door and stepped out onto the deck into the sun light.

I received a round of applause for my efforts and couldn't help but break out laughing. We were all still laughing as I sank into a comfortable deck chair next to a table full of crackers, cheese, pistachio nuts, sliced apples, a bowl of fruit, oj, apple juice. "Wow! This is living!" I exclaimed as I took in a great lungful of salt air.

"Yeah, you can see why we would never pass up our annual visit," said Mary who was lying on a big beach towel on the deck, smiling up at me.

"So, Sleeping Beauty, you sure look well-rested," Bill said.

"Oh, I am, thank you, but I'm afraid I haven't been much of a house guest."

"Actually, the perfect houseguest," Hilly said wickedly. "I hardly knew you were here! You certainly haven't been any trouble!" she added gaily.

"I know differently," I responded, "And, Hilly, thank you so much for everything!"

"You're so very welcome, I'm sure. I was…we were," she corrected, "…really afraid we'd never get to see you again," she said seriously.

"You almost didn't," I responded and that's all it took. From that point, I told Mary, Hilly and Bill everything— about running into the Gingerman… ah Slade, at Lum's after they left, the *Victoria E.*, Bish, Paddy, the wonderful spontaneous sailing venture, beach picnic, bloody dinghy, and waking up in the hospital in Portland. I even told them about Sir Walter, his wife and their story.

"Wow, Evie, what an exciting life you lead!" said Mary.

"Well," I hesitated and added, "I guess. But I really wish I knew how exciting. I mean I can't remember my last hours on the Bristol. I don't know what's happened to Paddy, Bish, Slade, the *Victoria E.*… I'm really afraid."

"There, there," Hilly soothed. "Don't you worry about a thing. We'll find out. I'm a master sleuth, really. I love mysteries. I'll make some calls to our friends in Nassau and have them check with people they know around the islands. We'll get to the bottom of this—it's better you don't use your name anyway, until we know what we're dealing with…. Don't worry Evie. We're just glad you're okay!

"Excuse me, everyone. I'll just go inside and make some calls—get the ball rolling at least." Hilly said as she got up and started into the cottage. Then she turned and added, "Eat, eat," as she strode on long, tan legs through the door.

"I mean it," she said, speaking from the other side of the screen door. "I'm not going to lose you to starvation after the ordeal you've been through. IVs… eck!" she made a face at us and was gone.

I ate and drank. Even when I was full I kept nibbling at the cheese and sipping apple juice.

Bill and Mary took turns filling me in on their spring and summer, and said that Lexy was doing great. "Thankfully, she was able to put that whole bad experience behind her and move on," Mary concluded soberly.

Hilly returned nearly half-an-hour later. She brought a great straw hat and sunglasses and passed them to me.

"Ummm, great. Thank you, Hilly. What did you find out?" I asked, turning to her and half rising in expectation of learning about my lost friends.

"Well, it's curious. I have some good sources—people who usually know something about everything, and no one…no one," she repeated, "has heard word one."

"No!—I can't believe that!" Mary and Bill exclaimed together. They were just as interested as I to hear what had happened.

"I'm afraid so. I'm sorry, Evie. But don't give up. These people are going to get back in touch with people they know who have access to, ah, such information," she said vaguely.

"Authorities?" I asked.

"Yes, and ah, others, too," she added mysteriously.

"If there's any way to know what's happened I'm sure they will dig it up. Oops, bad choice of words," she apologized, coloring slightly.

"Okay." Bill broke in. "Then if there's no more to be done on that front for now, let's get out of the house and show Evie the island."

"Hear, Hear!" Mary, the cheerleader, exclaimed.

"Are you up to it, Evie?" Hilly, the mother and *hostess extraordinaire*, asked me.

"Yes, I believe I'd like that. Actually, it would be wonderful," I responded, thinking how ironic it was I should feel so alive after nearly dying—that I ever even wanted to die—it was beyond me what I could have been thinking in that Ohio farmhouse attic nearly a lifetime ago. *Look at all I would have missed*, I marveled. I never wanted to die as long as there were people like Sir Walter and the teachers and Slade and....

"Walk or ride?" Hilly asked.

"Walk," I answered when everyone looked at me expectantly.

"Well, then, you'll need shoes, I mean sneakers or something more suitable than those flip-flops," Hilly said, "Come inside and we'll find you something from the cottage stock."

"We'll bring this in and then we're all set," Mary spoke for Bill, too.

The island was beautiful and the climate was so much more comfortable for me than the tropics. I much preferred the crisp, salty air to that searing, baking heat of the Caribbean, I realized.

Everything was wonderfully heightened like I'd just gotten senses or something. I could actually taste the salt in the air, smell the fresh cut grass or earthiness of the woods. I heard the screech of seagulls and the buzz of pollen-passing bees, as though I was really hearing for the first time in my life. Flowers smelled so sweet it nearly brought tears to my eyes, and the contrast of sky blues with sea blues and forest greens completed the visceral picture. At this time, I was newly aware of all this and it was indescribable.

The smell and squish of hot tar under my feet as we walked arm-in-arm down the deserted road seemed to heighten my remaining senses. At this moment, I thought this was the most heavenly place on earth. I wished I were with Slade. I was interested in sharing my thoughts and feelings, and I wanted to know if he'd experience the same overwhelming awareness and be moved as I was or was I just over-reacting because of my recent trauma.... Or was he so worldly that his impressions would be different—would he even care to be with me? Was he even alive?

"Evie, Evie, are you okay?" Hilly's concerned question caught my attention.

"Oh, ah," I smiled sheepishly. "You caught me daydreaming," I confessed. "This is just heaven on earth, this Sterling Island, Hilly. Thank you so much for inviting me!"

"Slade," she whispered conspiratorally.

I nodded and glanced at Bill and Mary happily engaged in conversation. They were walking along, arm-in-arm, in their own little world. I wondered....

"Hey, you know what?" Hilly asked.

"What?"

"What?"

"What?" I chimed in.

"The Club is having a dance tonight. What say we all get gussied up and go? The theme is a Senior Prom—doesn't that sound like fun?" Hilly asked excitedly.

"Gussied up?" I asked.

"Oh yeah," Hilly laughed, "nothing too fancy but shirt and tie for the men and dresses for the girls. You know, *gussied up.* Don't worry, we've got you covered."

"I know, I know," joining in the excitement, "the cottage stock!"

"Right you are, Evie. The cottage stock is all the odds and ends out-grown or left unclaimed by former guests— hats, shoes, slickers, tennis rackets, bathing suits. Why, Evie, we even have a prom dress that I think will be quite fetching on you!" Hilly laughed and then giggled for some time.

"It was, it was," she tried to explain but then just broke into fits of laughter as she remembered details of the story she wanted to relate. Her laughter was so infectious, we all just stopped in the middle of the deserted road and looked at Hilly and howled.

I almost wet myself. I could just imagine what we looked like—thank goodness no one came along. I'm quite sure they'd have mistaken us for escapees from some asylum.

"Another time, I guess," Hilly said between snorts of laughter. "I just, I just can't—well, not just now," she got out before succumbing to another burst of laughter.

"We've got the idea," Mary said. We needed her to stop laughing—our sides were killing us.

I was having the best time and didn't know why. I had nothing…no brooch, no assets, no money to speak of.... I didn't have a lover and three people I cared about had disappeared mysteriously without a trace. Yet, I was really happy and it dawned on me slowly like the morning sun rising in the east. I was happy inside. I was okay deep down and satisfied with who I was—the 'me in me' and that seemed to be the 'why.' The only thing different in my life, an aspect I never even knew was missing…the key ingredient was finally present. Things, other people, accomplishments, successes—well, all those things were well and good but you had to like yourself and not depend on others to find happiness. It seemed so simple, so obvious, now that I had the answer. I shook my head in wonder. I was startled out of my reverie when Bill spoke.

"The dance?" Bill asked.

"The dance," Mary said.

"The dance! Yes!" I exclaimed

"The dance, it is," Hilly confirmed and like the days we spent arm-in-arm in Nassau on our way to Lum's, we sang *Yellow Submarine* like we'd been doing it for years. Like Dorothy and her companions in The *Wizard of Oz*, we walked four abreast down the still-deserted road on our way back to Hilly's.

We soon tired. Laughing and tripping over ourselves and each other, we untangled and trudged on. It was getting hot.

"Okay, what's everyone want for dinner?" Hilly asked as she led us to her cottage down the back road and through the woods on a short path. We negotiated a large boulder that separated her house from the back yard and we stepped one by one onto the submarine deck.

"How 'bout roast chicken?" Hilly asked without waiting for anyone to answer her first question. "Yep, be done in about an hour—just enough time for cocktail hour on the screened in porch."

"What a life," I marveled again.

As we sat or rather lounged around on the furniture of the screened-in porch, I thought that this must be what it's like for people cruising on huge, luxury liners. Hilly's front yard was ocean and it wasn't hard to imagine Hilly as the tan, young, superb cruise director. We were the fortunate beneficiaries. The porch was cool with a frisky ocean breeze coming off the water. We could hear the large deck flag flapping against the flagpole. We heard people on the water sailing, kayaking or rowing by us, looking up at the magnificent cottage.

"Hilly," Mary asked. "When on earth did you put the chicken on?"

"Oh, I did it while I was on the phone," she winked. "I

was on hold a couple of times," she joked with Mary.

God, that chicken smells good, I thought. Hilly sure was right about the sea air and the healthy appetite! I was awed by Hilly's command of herself and her world. She must be something in the classroom, I realized.

"To Hilly."

"To Hilly."

"To Hilly. Hear, hear. The best hostess on land or sea," we toasted our hostess.

This reminded me of something but I wasn't sure what or why. My recollections were still unclear. It seemed my mind was still not recovered from my recent ordeal and something kept returning my thoughts to it.

The roast chicken dinner was delicious. We ate at the old family dining table overlooking the harbor. It was just growing dusky and various lights were beginning to appear on the water and neighboring islands. Conversation was minimal as everyone ate and envisioned their evening attire.

We cleared the table, put food away, dishes in the dishwasher, etc. then everyone disappeared to shower and prepare for the evening. I was sitting on the bed in the guestroom, looking out at the water when there was a soft tap at the door.

"Evie, can I come in?"

"Of course, Hilly," I said and pulled the bathrobe tight around me.

"Evie, look at these. Anything here appeal? Don't be afraid to tell me. I have lots more where these came from." Hilly was standing there with an armful of clothes. She spread them carefully on the bed beside me. "What do you think?"

I chose a crisp, white, short sleeve shirt and navy wraparound skirt. *Cottage stock, my foot*, I thought as I appraised the clothes but I said nothing.

"I can wear the white Speri Topsiders with that, don't you think?" I asked excitedly. I was referring to the thick sneaker-like canvas pull-ons I'd found and worn walking earlier in the day. They were so comfortable. Guess I was getting old, I thought to myself as I realized I'd chosen comfort over fashion appeal.

I smiled sheepishly at Hilly but she grinned back at me and said, "Yes, perfect. I've got a navy cardigan or blazer— either one will look great and keep you comfy. It gets quite nippy at night here, Evie."

Then she looked at me seriously and sat down beside me on the bed.

"You know, I'm very glad you're here. Everything will be okay so try not to worry," she said simply.

"I can't help but worry because I don't know what happened aboard the *Victoria E.* that last night. I can't even imagine. And where is Slade? What about Paddy and Bish? How come not one of your contacts heard a thing about the Bristol 48 and its crew, Hilly? It just doesn't make sense that such a big, beautiful boat would disappear with three people without so much as a whimper."

"Be patient, Evie. I know it seems surreal but the Caribbean, from my experience anyway, is sometimes a little backwards when it comes to sharing information. It's better than it was even a few years ago but I suspect that political problems could be involved here. Did you know that whole incident with Lexy was entirely suppressed for fear it would incite the white Bahamians and impact tourism? Not a word appeared in print or in the local TV news…. Columbus told me that today when I asked him to look into your situation.

184

"Really?" I asked, although I wasn't actually surprised.

"Yes. You must have known I'd call Columbus."

"I guess so but we were so far from Nassau and Paradise Island I didn't think about those connections, I guess. I don't know. I've just been so mixed up and so worried about everything. Except for our last day together, we were usually alone or on deserted islands and beaches. We rarely even saw another boat while we were on the water."

"Hmmmmm"

"I'm sorry, Hilly. I just wanted you to know, you know. I'm just happy to be here with you and Mary and Bill, too, of course. I can't think of anyone else who could help me get through this and show me such a wonderful time in the process."

Hilly took my hands in hers. "Good," she smiled. "We'll get through it together. Meanwhile, we'll enjoy ourselves and each other. Deal?"

"Deal," I agreed.

"Okay, then. See you downstairs when you are ready," she said and was gone.

I thought about what she said as I dressed. Nothing made sense but I had a feeling that Hilly would find the answers if it were humanly possible. With no strength, no money and no connections, there was nothing I could contribute outside of telling all I knew about Slade and my *Victoria E.* companions and our chemistry and fun time together. She would know how to use that information which is more than I could do under the circumstances. "Without Hilly, I wouldn't even have a roof over my head!" I whispered to my reflection in the mirror of the empty room.

I was determined to take Hilly's advice because it was the only practical thing to do, but also I didn't want to ruin everyone's annual reunion because of my ordeal. Still, I left the room with a heavy heart and somber mood and headed downstairs to join the noisy group who'd gathered in the kitchen with their drinks.

"Perfect," Mary exclaimed, smiling and pointing at me.

Everyone turned to check out my outfit and Hilly excused herself to get the navy blazer. Bill and Mary each handed me an Amstel Beer.

"Oh brother," I exclaimed, laughing, "two-at-a-time. I'm in real trouble, I think."

"Better get with it, kid," Mary said.

"Oh yes. I know I'm not in your league yet, but you'll be relieved to know that I'm going to work on it." I held my bottle up in a mock toast and the others cheered and joined in.

I laughed, too, surprising myself. These people just lightened my heart and their laughter was infectious.

Hilly returned with a handsome blazer, another unlikely cottage cast-off.

By the time we were piling into the wagon, beers in coolers, we were just four good friends on our way to a club dance, not a care in the world.

When we arrived a few minutes later, we had trouble finding a parking spot.

"Good crowd," Hilly mumbled as she finally selected a parking spot under an apple tree away from the rest of the cars.

Immediately there was a loud thump right above my head on the roof of the car. I jumped out as I let out a squeal of surprise.

"Just an apple," Hilly said nonchalantly. "Just another dent in the old war wagon."

"Well, I can see why nobody parked here," Bill teased.

"Okay, guests. Grab your refreshments and follow me." Hilly led the way to the Club House door and stood first in line talking with one of the people sitting at a table near the entrance.

Hilly reached in her pocket and pulled out a bill, which she passed to the woman next to the door. "Thanks, Jane," she said and reached back and the first woman stamped the back of her hand.

"All set you guys," she said as she stepped aside graciously.

Each of us in turn offered a hand for stamping.

Just as we stepped into the huge dimly lit room, a band began to play. To our right was an elevated stage with five band members bobbing and weaving to *Louie, Louie*. They were pretty good, I thought.

I turned back around and found myself standing alone. I squinted to see where Hilly, Mary and Bill had gone.

"They're right over there. See—in the corner,"

Hilly was waving away.

"Oh yes, I see, thank you, ah...."

"M—" I couldn't hear what he said but I recognized him as the lobsterman I thought fell on me when the Casco Bay boat landed upon my arrival here. "Oh, ah, yes. Thank you again."

"I hope you'll save a dance for me," he said politely.

I didn't know what to say. It was the last thing I expected to hear from him.

"Sure," I said and thought, *Why not?* as I headed to where Hilly was still standing and waving.

Our little group took up the end of a large wooden table that sat twelve.

Hilly was busy handing out beers from the cooler. "I brought some glasses if anyone's interested," she added.

Nobody was interested in a glass it seemed.

"This is BYOB and I know most of the people here. Actually grew up with half of them, if you can believe that! Anyway, I can probably arrange a trade if someone wants something else to drink," she concluded.

No one wanted anything else to drink.

Hilly then introduced us to the others at the table. Obviously she had made these arrangements in advance and her island friends were holding these seats for her.

I stood and said, "Nice to meet you," and sat down. Mary and Bill had obviously met these people on previous visits and after saying their hellos were busy looking at the people on the dance floor.

I sipped my beer and watched everyone having a good time doing the twist! Hilly was busily engaged in conversation with a fellow seated beside her. I think she introduced him as Rick. I wondered how he fit into her life. Soon, they got up and danced.

I was enjoying the music and watching all the dancers although I couldn't see them that clearly. But I was content listening to the music and thinking of nothing in particular. I was interrupted.

"Excuse me."

I turned to see the fisherman bending down beside me, a bottle of Bud in his hand. I held my breath. I really didn't feel like dancing.

"May I sit down?"

"Oh, okay, sure, have a seat," I stammered, relieved he hadn't asked me to join him on the dance floor.

He said something to me but I couldn't hear what he

was saying so I leaned closer to him.

"Would you like to go outside and get some fresh air?" he asked.

Without hesitation, I stood and pushed my chair out of the way. Mary and Bill were staring at me.

"Fresh air," I yelled, pointing toward the porch.

They smiled and nodded in unison.

My fisherman friend and I stepped outside onto the very old, large wooden porch and walked half-way around it. It looked like it encircled the building but actually went only three-quarters of the way around. We stood leaning on the railing, which was like a mini-wall—solid and comfortable.

"Hot in there," my new friend commented. It was beginning to be a problem with my not knowing his name.

"Ummm," I replied.

"So you're a friend of Hildegarde's? Are you one of her students?"

"No," I laughed.

"Teach with her then?"

"No, I met Hilly when we stayed at the same motel on vacation. She invited me to visit her when she hosted this annual reunion. I'm glad I did—it's wonderful here."

"I'm glad, too." His so-blue eyes sparkled in the porch light.

"So, what do you do on Sterling's Island," I asked, not wanting to talk about myself.

"I'm a fisherman," he replied. "Actually, I lobster."

"Lobster? So you catch lobsters?"

"Um, yeah. Trap 'em really."

"You know, I haven't got the slightest idea how all that works. Is it hard to find lobsters?"

He looked at me quizzically. "Where are you from anyway?" he asked.

"The midwest. We don't have salt air or salt water and no lobsters where I come from. And, this is my first time in Maine."

"Oh, I see. Well, my grandfather and father lobstered and I've been doing it since I was oh so big," he held his hand about mid-thigh-high.

"That young?"

"Yes," he quipped. "Anyway, I grew up lobstering so I know all the good spots. I do all right," he smiled slyly. I sensed that was an understatement though I didn't know why. There was something in the way he said it and the look he gave me afterwards.

"You can earn a living?" I asked.

"Yip." His voice was at least two octaves higher than his normal speaking voice. For some reason, I giggled and that made him break out in a great booming laugh. "I'm curious, fascinated.... Where do you find the lobsters? How many do you get in a day? How long does it take?"

"Whoa, whoa there, little girl, slow down now. One question at a time, please."

Did he say, *little girl?* No one had ever called me that before. I giggled again. I didn't believe it for a moment, but I sure liked the sound of it!

I was over forty and this guy was, well, maybe twenty-five or thirty and could have been my son if I'd started a family very early in life. The thought gave me goosebumps. *What made me think of that?* I asked myself, disgusted.

I had no romantic interest in this young fisherman but I did find his attention flattering. I liked his shy demeanor, emboldened by Budweiser, I imagined. Nonetheless I found

I was enjoying his company, relaxed in his presence, and I wanted to know more about lobstering.

"Okay, why don't you go out with me—lobstering," he added quickly.

"When?" I asked, excited at the prospect of seeing this occupation first-hand.

"Oh, I don't know, anytime. How about tomorrow?"

"Maybe... What time? Where?"

"I could meet you here. See that float?" He pointed to a wooden structure floating on the water in front of the club house "You just follow the walkway underneath where we are standing and go down the ramp and you're there. I'll be waiting in my boat, *The Rose*, it's grey and white."

"What time?"

"Well, I go out around 4 so..."

"Four in the morning—4 a.m.?" I asked incredulously.

I was talking so loudly that other people on the porch turned to look at me. Mary, Bill and Hilly were there, too, watching me.

"Yes," he said with a little laugh, quite amused at my reaction to the time...a time that he didn't give a second thought to since he'd been doing it all his life.

"But I can go out and haul some traps and work my way in this direction so I could pick you up say eight or nine," he added quickly when he saw my expression.

"I'd like to go. Eight would be fine. I'm from a farm family and getting up early is in my blood too. It's just that I haven't done it in so long, I guess I overreacted. I just have to check with my hostess and make sure she doesn't mind or have other plans, you know...."

"Oh, no, Evie. You go. You'll have a great time! Micah's the best!"

His name is Micah, I thought with some relief.

It was Hilly. She, Mary and Bill had been sitting in rocking chairs at the corner of the porch when I'd spotted them earlier but now they were standing beside us, smiling.

"Sure, Hilly here has gone with me a couple of times," Micah laughed. "She's an old pro—a boat person from way back."

"That's a compliment, I guess," Hilly shot back at Micah.

"A-yah," an exaggerated 'Down East' expression with a grin and a wink.

"Well, ah, sure then I'll be on the float at...."

"Or I can pick you up at Hilly's?"

"What?" I asked thinking that was too much to expect from him to lobster for 3 or 4 hours and then tie up his boat and, drive down and pick me up and then go back out to finish his day's work with me as an observer.

"Yeah, you be on the rocks in front of Hilly's at 8 a.m. sharp. The tide will be high around then—no problem," he finished.

"Well, all right, I guess." I looked at Hilly who nodded.

"Yep. Then it's all set. Now we're going home—gonna call it a day," Hilly said, glancing at Mary and Bill who nodded in agreement.

"Okay," I said. "What time is it anyway?"

"Not quite 10," Hilly replied glancing at her watch.

"I could—" Micah started, and then said, "—okay, then, see you at 8 a.m. sharp."

"Yes, good night then. Thank you." I looked at Micah, who was smiling at the four of us. I wasn't sure why I'd thanked him.

"Good music," Mary commented as we made our way to the parking lot.

"Yes, they're a local group but they are very, very popular. We try and get them at least twice a summer. We have to book a year in advance." Hilly told us.

We all piled into the wagon.

"Hey, where's Bill?" Mary asked and then said, "Here he comes. He's got your cooler, Hilly."

Hilly laughed. "I forgot all about that! Thanks, Bill."

"Welcome, Hilly," replied Bill as he climbed into the backseat with Mary.

The ride home was quiet and fast. It was only a few minutes from the Club to Hilly's by car. It took as long to walk the winding path to Hilly's as it did to drive to the parking lot at Hilly's circle.

We trudged along the path fairly well-lit by several street lights, then up the long staircase at Hilly's

"Ugh," Mary groaned. "I'm beat."

"Me too," Bill agreed.

I didn't have the strength to say anything. I was trying to catch my breath.

"Anyone hungry?" Hilly, the consummate hostess sang out.

"Oh no," I exclaimed and didn't know why.

"Bed, bed, then," Hilly said, when Mary and Bill said, "No" and "Couldn't", respectively.

One-by-one we filed up the stairs. Hilly was last after she turned out the lights. There was a flurry of activity as everyone readied themselves for bed then everything was quiet except for the waves lapping at the rocks below and the bell buoy in the nearby channel.

"Hilly," I asked over the partition that separated the guest room from hers. "Did you really go lobstering with Micah?"

"Yeah, did you Hilly? When?" It was Mary from her room on the other side of Hilly.

No one had closed their doors but the walls of the rooms were only so high and with little effort we could easily talk amongst ourselves. The one room upstairs that was totally enclosed was the bathroom.

"Oh, years ago and I didn't lobster, I just watched. I no longer had a lobster license so I wasn't allowed to do anything but observe then. I'd lobstered when I was a little girl. I had six traps and a row boat. Things were simpler in those days."

"Why'd you stop?"

"Oh, I don't know. Found boys, took up tennis, sailing. Taught swimming at the Club. Pretty soon I didn't have time to get the bait, let alone do justice to my little enterprise."

"How big was your little enterprise? Did you sell them?" Bill again.

"Oh, no," Hilly laughed. "I just did it because it was fun and my family loved lobster. I only had enough traps to guarantee a good Sunday dinner, usually. Sometimes I had extras that I gave to friends, but that was a rare occurrence."

"Gosh, it sounds so neat. Like something out of a children's book or some romantic story about the beautiful young girl who lived on a Maine island and…." Mary said but was interrupted by Bill.

"What a wonderfully fun thing to do, Hilly. Who knew?"

"Ha, ha," Hilly laughed. "Well, it was, of course, most of the time but believe me, it was a lot of work, too. And there was nothing romantic about lugging those big heavy traps around and the bait was awful. Well, there's just nothing romantic about bait."

"Didn't you miss it?" I asked, laughing about the bait remark.

"What?"

"You know, didn't you miss it? After a while, I mean. Didn't you miss lobstering?"

"Oh sure. Eventually, I did want to get back into it but things had really changed. They were using wire traps and they were very expensive. And, the license was very costly and you had to have time as a stern man on somebody's boat. Aside from the expense it was very time-consuming to buy everything and keep it repaired and running. I don't know, in the end it was just easier to spend the day with one of the locals when I got the urge to be on the water in a lobster boat. Usually, I'm content to watch them in my front yard while I sun myself on the rocks," she added.

For a while Mary, Bill and I took turns asking questions about lobstering, Hilly's experiences, etc. Then it was just me and Mary.

Soon, it was just me asking questions. I had so many and I was so excited about the next morning, but I was soon overtaken, too, and dropped off to sleep.

CHAPTER TWENTY-FOUR

I slept soundly despite my anticipation. I could smell bacon and hear voices downstairs. It was already light out! I jumped out of bed afraid I'd missed Micah! Quickly, I glanced at the clock in Hilly's room. Seven o'clock exactly, I realized with relief that I hadn't overslept.

"Oh good," I sighed. "Plenty of time..." Hilly had told me last night to wear old clothes and not to bother showering. She said I'd surely need to bathe when I returned from a day on the lobster boat.

I scurried across to the bathroom, a little lame from yesterday's exercise but fit enough, I judged, to withstand today's planned activity. I threw cold water in my face. "Eeek," I exclaimed as the frigid Sebago Lake water hit me full in the face.

"Bracing!" I said to the mirror.

I ran a comb through my hair, brushed my teeth and returned to the bedroom. I closed the door behind me, threw off the nightclothes and surveyed the borrowed wardrobe to see if I could find something suitable for lobstering. I gave up and ended up putting on the clothes I went walking in the day before.

Who cares? I asked myself as I set the shades and made the bed. I looked around the room to be sure it was presentable and when I determined it was, I hurried downstairs.

The huge dining room table was covered with a lovely white-with-green cross stitched antique table cloth. There was orange and grapefruit juice—two domed plates, English Muffins and toast, a chaffing dish full of scrambled eggs, a platter of thick slab bacon and Country Ham, a small jar of imported marmalade, milk, coffee...

"Oh my gosh!" I exclaimed. "A meal fit for a farmer! What is going on here? It looks like you're having Sunday brunch or something?"

"Hilly was hungry," Bill said and everyone broke out in fits of laughter.

"Oh Bill, honestly now," Mary said, pretending to be exasperated by his constant teasing.

"Actually, there's a good explanation for all of this." Hilly waved her arm over the table.

"Always is...when Hilly's involved," Bill again.

"Everyone woke up hungry."

"Starved," Mary agreed.

"And we all just started grabbing things and pretty quick, well you see the results. Let's dig in while it's still hot. Your timing is perfect, Evie! Now sit down." A half hour later we were still picking at the bacon and sipping coffee—close to bursting but not able to stop eating, not wanting to move.

"Salt air?" I asked.

"We warned you," Mary said, giggling.

"True, you did, but I never believed I could have such a ferocious appetite!"

"Aha, I hear diesel engines," Hilly interrupted our banter.

"Oh no, he's early!" I exclaimed.

"Yep, it's Micah," Hilly confirmed as she slid open the glass slider on the poop deck and waved to him.

"Ah, wait a minute! What do I need? Anything?"

"Here, Evie." Hilly handed me a medium sized canvas sack with a draw-string tie. "Sun tan lotion, etc.," she said and put her hand on my arm.

"Here's a sweatshirt in case you get cold out back."

"Oh Hilly, you're too much! You think of everything! What would we do without you? Thank you, Hilly. Thank you so much."

"Have fun!" Mary said.

"Good fishin'," Bill added.

"See you for cocktails anyway. Invite Micah if you want."

I hurried out the back door, around the corner and down the long flight of steps.

I could see Micah sitting on the side of his boat with his feet resting on one of the rocks in front of Hilly's. He looked as natural as could be—like he'd been fending boats off rocks all his life and I guessed he probably had. It was quite a sight. I glanced over my shoulder and saw my friends on the deck above, watching.

"Hey, good morning, come aboard," he was grinning ear-to-ear. I couldn't help it, I grinned back at him, delighted to be going on this big adventure.

For a moment I stood on one leg like a crane poised on a rock, with one foot pointing toward the rail on the boat.

For an instant, I thought of the disastrous outcome this could have, and with every one watching. "Oh Lord," I said under my breath.

Big, strong arms plucked me from the rock and in a split second I was aboard. I didn't know what had happened, it was so fast.

Then I was standing on the deck of *The Rose* looking up, up, up at Hilly's impressive 'cottage' rising from the ledge like a fortress above us.

Hilly, Mary, and Bill were standing on the small 'poop-deck' beside the long, screened-in porch. They whistled and waved—my own cheering section, the best anyone could ask for. Micah threw the engines in gear and the boat charged through the channel and into the open ocean beyond.

The sun had been up for hours and it was quite comfortable until we passed from the island's protective mass and then it was downright chilly. I silently thanked Hilly for the added sweatshirt as I pulled it on.

"Ah, you came prepared! I'm impressed!" Micah yelled above the roar of the engines.

"Hilly," I yelled by way of explanation.

He nodded his understanding and smiled at me before turning his attention to the waters ahead. *Out back,* I guessed from my lobstering lesson from Micah on the porch at the dance, and Hilly once everyone had settled down the night before.

I was anxious for the experience and to put my new-found knowledge to use.

CHAPTER TWENTY-FIVE

I looked around the deck under and around Micah as he steamed to where his traps were set. My first thought was that this was a setting to make a marine biologist smile. Tidy as the boat was, I could see remnants from the hours Micah had pulled traps before he'd picked me up. Everywhere I looked I could see skeletons of small sea life. I saw baby crabs and tiny shrimp-like critters, snails, crushed or sun-baked crabs; periwinkles and bits of barnacles hugged the rails and corners of *The Rose.*

As I cautiously examined the bait barrel, I held my breath in anticipation of what Hilly told me was the awful stench of rotting redfish bait. Finally, I had to inhale and I did slowly, ready now to be overwhelmed by the putrid smell. Nothing. I sniffed again, bolder this time, still no assault to my nostrils.

I looked up to see Micah watching me, bemusement in his eyes. I thought I'd been totally discreet but I hadn't fooled him for a minute. He nodded and winked, his blue eyes crinkled in the bright, early morning sun.

"Pogies, heavily salted," was all he said.

He was different now, changed from the evening before. He was all business—a man from a fishing family with a lifetime of experience in the ways of the Atlantic and how to make a living from it. He was all strength and efficiency and I could tell that he made compromises only as a last resort. I sensed that he would push himself and his boat to the very limit but not to the point of recklessness. He'd go close though, very close—I could read it in the sun-baked lines of his face, the steel in his eyes and the set of his jaw.

He was a powerful man yet I was hardly aware of that fact because of his general demeanor, but there was no denying it. He pulled on a pair of well-worn cotton gloves and began grabbing the salty twisted bodies of the bait fish, three at a time. His strong, practiced hands thrust the bait into the nylon mesh bag. A nylon drawstring pulled taut closed the bait bag.

"Least favorite part," he mumbled when he saw me watching him in fascination. The salt from the bait fish flew off as he roughly but expertly handled them. The salt stung my eyes and I wiped them frequently.

"Can I help?" I asked hopefully. I half wanted him to say no, I think.

He smiled a knowing smile.

"Gloves in the Playmate cooler," he said and guided me as I fumbled to a couple of different coolers in the wheel house.

Finally, I located the right Playmate. He'd never stopped working while I found the new gloves and put them on. To my amazement they fit perfectly. *A good omen?* I wondered to myself.

"Buy them by the gross?" I couldn't resist yelling.

"By the dozen," he responded automatically.

He made it look so easy. I copied his movements. The fish were stiff, cold and uncooperative. They fell from my unskilled hands back into the bait barrel. He made it look so easy. The nylon bags were also uncooperative. They didn't want to conform to the fish and even when I was able to push the pogies into the flattest part of the bag, they somehow managed to jump out or a tail or a head—something— protruded from the bag, making it impossible to close. I glanced at the huge bait barrel and then Micah, who was pretending to watch what he was doing but he was grinning—he'd seen me struggling with the bait bag task.

When Micah was satisfied he had enough bait bags to resume lobstering, he busied himself with other work. I pressed on with my job, determined to master this bait bag thing. I persevered and actually did get better at it. I smiled to myself as I bent over the barrel. Soon my back was killing me and my clothes were covered in fish scales. I tried to ignore the situation. I was sure Micah withstood much more discomfort and on a regular basis. This, too, was in his eyes.

The boat lunged forward, then slammed into reverse and I was nearly pitched into the bait barrel. I damn near went over the rail when Micah next 'put it in the corner' and did a 360 degree turn.

"Rocks," was all Micah said.

Between lunges, I continued with my job.

I stole a glance at the captain. At some point he'd managed to pull on high rubber pants. They were bright orange and had a bib and wide shoulder straps. He wore thick rubber boots, black. He was a professional and as much a master of his boat as an Indy race car driver was his formula one speedster.

Harsh sun and salt air parched my lips but I wouldn't have missed this for the world. I licked my lips and tasted the salt—a very different sensation from the usual lipstick or gloss that my tongue found there.

"That's enough for now." He startled me out of my daydreaming. He stood beside me. The boat was moving forward with no one at the wheel. He was unconcerned as the boat cut through the water as though he steered her through sheer will. It was like *The Rose* was on automatic pilot. Could it be that lobster boats could be controlled telekinetically or did they have automatic pilots like planes? *I'd have to ask.*

With ease, Micah lifted the heavy box filled with bait bags. He placed it carefully atop the box where a few pogies remained unbagged. Somehow I had managed to make a dent in the supply. I wondered if I'd managed to help in some small way. Was my presence a pleasant diversion or was it a hindrance that had to be tolerated since he'd given his word to take me?

I took my place on the stool that he indicated, which was in the shelter of the wheel house, and he got down to the real business of lobstering. We fairly flew from buoy to buoy. All the traps between buoys—a string—were pulled from the bottom of the sea by an electric winch by the helm. I had the distinct impression the sea did not part with its bounty willingly.

But the sea was generous today in that it gave Micah more than he wanted: mud, periwinkles, urchins, eel grass, seaweed, small crabs and other sea life littered the rail.

Lobsters twitched and protested as they were hauled from the trap, checked for size, sex and eggs then banded or thrown back into the sea depending on how they presented themselves.

The radio sputtered every now and then. Sometimes I could make out pieces of conversation, other times I could not. The engine made varying noises as she went forward, increased speed, or slowed, 'rested' in neutral.

Every now and again I heard the splash of a too-small or too-big lobster or a sculpin being returned to the sea. Seagulls would occasionally light on the side of the boat when it was still and take off and follow it from trap to trap. Sometimes they'd land on the bow watching as I did, but for different reasons. When Micah returned some things to the sea, a quick and vigilant gull would swoop down and grab the bounty before it had a chance to swim away or sink back to the bottom.

It was chilly but Micah worked in a flannel shirt and sweatshirt, sleeves rolled up to the elbow. He wore the same dirty, wet gloves he'd stuffed the bait bags with... I couldn't help thinking that I could stand the dirty gloves but the wet part would not be acceptable to me. Micah didn't seem to notice.

The radio—WBLM—blared in the background making an eerie punctuation to the whine and whir of engines, winches, and VHF as Micah worked.

Lobster tails flipped in frustration at the battle lost. Movement was restricted as thick rubber bands clamped the claws—a tearing claw and a thicker crushing claw—shut. I'd learned that this measure was necessary in order to keep the lobsters from injuring themselves or each other. This expensive cargo would be delivered in perfect shape for the market and the pot.

After a couple of hours of his routine, Micah removed a Lemon-Lime Gatorade from the white and blue Playmate by Igloo.

He took a gulp, never missing a beat with the throttle, gears, winch control, measuring, cleaning or baiting process that was as much a part of his life as breathing.

I noticed he never stood on the tangled coil of rope at his feet, beneath the winch. He came close to that potentially deadly hemp by resting one booted foot atop it but his weight was on the other foot with solid deck beneath it. I supposed it wouldn't matter if a lobsterman could swim, although Hilly said a surprising number could not. A person with heavy rubber knee boots with the rubber pants wouldn't stand a chance if he was dragged over the stern and caught in the lines as the brick-laden traps made their way to the bottom. The boat would move ahead as trap after trap would be pulled from the stern behind the hapless fisherman.

Involuntarily I shuddered as I imagined the experience I remembered as it had been told to me the night before. Somehow it hadn't seemed real then or so sinister and hopeless. Now I could see that it was both. Even though most fishermen carried a knife in their boot for just such an occurrence, it didn't seem like they'd stand a chance....

As I watched the fascinating processes involved in lobstering, "In a gadda da vita, baby" or something like that was blaring from the radio, the winch was grinding and the engine was idling while the wheelhouse wall vibrated behind my back. Seagulls screeched overhead and I could smell pine and salt air and mud and sea life fill my nostrils; the sun warmed my hands. My senses were assailed from every angle and I was in heaven! I'd almost forgotten how much I enjoyed being on the water. I thought of Slade and quickly pushed his image from my mind.

I just can't think about him now, I told myself.

All the time the hauling continued, the boat seemed to

be working just as hard as Micah.

Somehow, miraculously, it seemed to know how to avoid the rocks, other buoys, other boats, etc. The winch, too, knew its job—stopping at the knot just before the trap, continuing in the interim. The winch was another great danger I'd heard about last evening. But it seemed now to be so innocent, functional, a huge help, as I watched it go about its work.

Suddenly it dawned on me that Micah was subtly controlling the progress of the winch, the boat—his efforts were so fluid that his actions escaped my attention 'til now.

Micah tossed a newly picked and baited trap over the side. The rope near his feet untangled more and more rapidly as more traps followed in a domino effect. Soon all the traps are gone and Micah took another swig of Gatorade as he made his way to the next black and yellow buoy— colors that are registered to him and signify these are his traps.

As the winch ground through the next set of traps, I was sprayed by the cold salt water as it was pulled with the line into the boat, onto the railing. And so it went, from one string to the next.

I noticed some horrible looking sponge-like stuff—it looked like an overgrowth of a turkey's comb. I don't know why but it reminded me of cancer—so odd and irregular is the proliferation of growth. Micah seemed unconcerned about its presence and ignored it, unlike the starfish, red crabs, sculpin and other things he nonchalantly returned to the sea before he placed a fresh bait bag in the trap, secured the door, and guided the trap to the stern to await its return to the sea.

I shifted on the stool in the corner of the wheelhouse. I was cold, thirsty and worst of all, I had to pee. I didn't want to think about that. I licked my dry lips, tried not to gag on the diesel fumes that now seemed to overwhelm me. I tried to distract myself from the growing discomfort so I watched the little red crabs scampering around or lying crushed under Micah's heavy black boots.

Micah worked tirelessly. I was about done in. My back ached, my bladder was full. I dreaded the next time we crossed another boat's wake and I'd be bounced around. *Will my bladder burst—will I embarrass myself? Micah? Soil the three layers of clothes and long johns Hilly had given me that I'm now wearing? I pray not.*

Just as Micah was bound to take me on this trip once he'd invited me, I was bound to see it to its conclusion. It was all he'd asked of me—that if I went with him, I went for the entire time—start to finish.

A small family of ducks swam one in front of the other, along the deserted shoreline. We passed the other end of the island, the exclusive end where the privileged come in June to while away the summer months with tennis, sailing, dances, bridge and endless rounds of cocktail parties. But now I wondered how people kept two houses, paid taxes, and upkeep on two residences. How could I have gone through life oblivious to so much? I shuddered again—this time it was not due to the cold but to my own ignorance, lack of awareness. I'd learned more about life in the last few months than in the forty plus years before....

Micah took a brush and scrubbed at the rail and deck, then splashed a pail of salt water over the remaining mud, etc., washing the area clean.

He'd taken off one wet glove and then he put it back on. Once again, I was moved by this. He obviously didn't think a thing of it but to me it was like torture—the height of discomfort. Was it just habit or did he do it to save money or did he use one glove until it fell apart like his ancestors before him?

Then Micah left his post by the rail, wheel and winch and leaned in front of me into the engine room. He fumbled around below and I noticed him open a big red toolbox. He grabbed pliers, knife, rope and he was back by the rail replacing line. He moved the trap to the stern.

It was colder now. The sun had retreated or been eclipsed by clouds. Another boat passed nearby, words were exchanged. I couldn't understand what had been said.

Micah worked on. He was unchanged, with the exception that his arms were now muddy between the gloves and elbows—the exposed area. This was dirty and hard work—dangerous, too. Yet there was something wild, refreshing and wonderful about it—unlike truck farming in Ohio. I decided I could do this work—love this life—if I were younger that is....

A song played in the background, *It's Good to be King*. I heard the lyrics and understood And I smiled, despite my discomfort. I was happy and I was loving this day.

Three hours and fifteen minutes into my day—fifteen minutes past noon, the little Playmate produced a frosty Busch. Fishing was also thirsty work; I discovered that watching fishing was too. But Micah looked at me, offering the Busch and I shook my head 'no' with a smile.

The water was calm, the wind too. The only breeze was created by our forward motion as we steamed... home? I can't imagine what it would be like out here when the ocean is rough, the wind howling, ice chunks floating around in the winter.

Today, the water was calm, the sun shone brightly and

the boat was again clean. We steamed home. I remember the lyrics *It's good to be king,* and I smiled again. I watched Micah's broad shoulders and capable form at the wheel. I thought he must feel like a king—so free¬, so in control and master of his own destiny.

Micah tied up at his float and helped me off *The Rose.* He gave me a ride to Hilly's in his bright red truck and I thanked him. He passed me a plastic bag and I asked if he'd like to join us for cocktails later this afternoon.

"Sure, that sounds perfect. I've got to go to town to sell the lobsters and pick up some bait, but I'll be back after that. Four good?"

"Great," I said and headed to Hilly's with my bags—I couldn't wait to tell her all about my day. I couldn't wait to get to the bathroom!

I waved to Micah and headed up the path

It is good to be king, I thought.

CHAPTER TWENTY-SIX

When I returned to Hilly's everyone was on the deck.

"How was it?" they asked in unison.

"Great!" I exclaimed. "I will tell you all about it when I get back from the bathroom!" I nearly shouted at them.

"Hilly, I have something from Micah in here." And I gave her the plastic bag, which she promptly took to the kitchen

I finally had a chance to pee in a toilet rather than the bucket Hilly had told me sufficed for the 'head' on a lobster boat. Then I grabbed a towel and some clothes and jumped into the shower. I couldn't believe no one commented on my wind-blown, mud-spattered appearance.

When I got in, I soaped up, washed my hair and let the lovely warm water cascade over my sore, tired, cold body. It was absolute heaven and I realized now why my mother had always said, "Cleanliness is next to Godliness, my dear." I had a momentary pang of loss as I remembered my loving mother and how much she cared for me when I was a little girl—and even a big girl.

Too bad you only get one mother in life, I thought. I quickly pushed the thought out of my head for I could feel myself tear up with thoughts of my family and the farm.

I dressed quickly in tan shorts and a yellow T-shirt and some moccasins I found under the bed. I ran a comb through my hair and put on some lip gloss—my lips were so chapped, I couldn't believe it.

I came downstairs and Hilly had made sandwiches and iced tea and everyone was relaxing on the deck, catching the midday sun and chatting. The scene was idyllic.

I grabbed a sandwich and in between bites I told them about my morning and all the excitement of lobstering in Casco Bay. They took turns asking questions and I did my best to tell them what I thought or remembered.

Once again, it was a thoroughly enjoyable meal with good company and great food. "Anybody for the Seagull's Roost?"

"The what?" I asked.

Oh, our favorite hangout down here is called the Seagull's Roost and we try to get down as often as possible. They have great mixed drinks and plenty of good company and everyone that is anyone gets off the CBL boat after working in town all day and comes in for a cold one."

"Oh, wow, I'd love to," I enthused. I had no idea where I was getting my energy or why I wanted so much to get out but I suspected I didn't want to think about the loss of my parents and Bounder and Slade and Paddy and Bish. Then I remembered Micah.

"But Micah is coming back for cocktails so I guess I'd better stay," I added regretfully.

"Well, don't worry, Micah will join us—he practically lives at the Roost! Ah, I think I hear him coming up the stairs; let's ask him."

"Hey."

"Hey, yourself. You want to join us for a cold one at the Roost?"

"What a question!"

"Okay, let's get ready and meet back here in five. Micah, there's beer in the fridge if you want to have a cold one while we collect our things."

"Ah don't mind if I do, thank you."

We all went into the house and everyone ran this way and that. Mary changed into a nice summer dress with a sweater over her shoulders.

"Too much?" she asked.

"You look terrific," I responded as I made my way into the bathroom.

I combed my hair and grabbed the blazer and my purse and headed back downstairs. I ran into everyone in the kitchen. Micah was still on the porch.

We went out and collected him. He left his empty bottle on the porch table and joined us.

"To the war wagon," Hilly yelled over her shoulder and we all followed her as she made her way down the path.

"I'll take my truck and meet you at the Roost," Micah said and was gone in a cloud of dust.

We all piled into Hilly's wagon and took off after him.

He was already inside by the time we parked beside his big red Ford in the parking lot behind the Roost.

I felt like a kid on another big adventure. *No matter where you were, life was good and fun when you with people you really enjoyed*, I thought.

We walked into the restaurant/bar. Hilly was first and I followed her and Mary and Bill brought up the rear.

"Ah, ha," Hilly laughed. "There you are, Micah. I expected to find you at your usual spot at the bar."

Everyone took a seat at the table Micah had selected for us. Hilly and Mary and Bill were passing the wine list around and perusing the drink menu, talking incessantly about what would taste good and what they wanted and when they last had what exotic drink. I was looking out the window, spellbound.

Micah must have seen my face because he started pointing out the various World War II forts and nearby islands. What a magnificent view from our perch! The Portland skyline was truly breathtaking. As lovely as Hilly's spot was, this was totally different but equally as exceptional.

I thought I heard my name but I was engrossed in Micah's descriptions of Sterling Island's early settlers and Indian raids.

When he stopped to catch his breath, I heard Hilly say everyone was having drafts and they'd ordered one for me if that was okay.

"Fine, thank you," I replied.

We all laughed and ate fried veggies and talked and Mary and Bill danced a little to the old juke box. Hilly found her friend Rick from the Club House dance last night and I sat listening to Micah and thoroughly enjoying myself.

People came and went and many of them stopped to have a word with Hilly and Rick.

I sat wondering what my future held with no assets and no real job skills. I looked at Hilly and Mary and Bill and thought that as much as I'd like to follow them back to college in the fall, I had nothing to offer the school. Micah was a lobsterman and I just learned that he was a firefighter in the city as well. Everyone had a job or jobs or were 'set' without one—comfortably retired or living on family money.

I had never worried about my future before or how I could earn a living; it was a strange thing to contemplate now, but I realized I would have to do it. *Ah, later*, I thought and the evening wore on.

Micah excused himself and disappeared into the now-teeming room.

As it got later, the lights came on then dimmed and the Portland skyline really lit up and was simply gorgeous. I looked around to see where Hilly had gone to so I could tell her how impressed I was with the beautiful sights here. I didn't see Hilly and I didn't see Mary and Bill or Micah.

I was alone, sipping my beer and contemplating my future.

Suddenly, a drink appeared on the table before me and I looked quizzically at the waitress.

"Some handsome man, you lucky dog," she said and turned away.

I looked at the huge crowd around the bar but couldn't make out anyone I knew or even recognized.

I turned back to watch the sunset and took a sip of the drink.

I stood immediately. *Who would buy me a CC and Ginger?*

I would recognize the drink anywhere and once again I scanned the people in the room, straining my eyes to see someone looking at me.

I felt someone behind me! Great arms encircled my shoulders, warm breath found my neck.

"What the... Who...?" and I whipped myself around and there I was staring into Slade's handsome face.

"Oh my Lord," I almost fainted. "Slade. What are you

doing here? Where have you been? How did you find me? Where are Paddy and Bish and the *Victoria E.*?" Everything came rushing out.

"Evie," he said and kissed me. He kissed me like I had never been kissed before. The music, the people, everything else ceased to exist. I thought someone had pulled a string at the pit of my stomach. I experienced this feeling for the first time in my life. He almost took my breath away. What a sensation—I'd almost forgotten the effect he had on me!

"Hi, Slade, I'm Hilly. I'm so glad I finally get to meet you. This is Mary and Bill—they are friends who teach with me in New Hampshire and are here for our annual reunion."

Thank the lord for Hilly—once again she'd come to my rescue. I could feel my face flush and I knew it must be scarlet; the hives on my neck were beginning to itch. I took another gulp of the CC and Ginger and tried to calm my nerves while introductions were made. Slade stood beside me and even when he shook Bill's hand, his arm stayed firmly around my shoulders. For a minute, I thought I'd died and gone to heaven, so overwhelmed with emotion I was— could my dream of true love be realized after all?

"Where are you staying, Slade? Would you like to join us at Grey Boulders? You could stay as long as you like, of course, and it wouldn't be a problem."

"Well, I took a room in Portland, but I'd love to stay here and catch up with Evie and spend time with you all, if it's not a problem."

"Nope, we'd be happy to have you," Hilly said.

"Well, I'm thrilled to meet you because I heard about all the effort you went to trying to find me and I owe you a huge thank you."

Slade squeezed me again. I was speechless.

"War wagon?" Bill asked and we all just followed him out the door to Hilly's car. I couldn't help notice that Micah's truck was gone.

Hilly put her arm in mine and Slade followed behind us up the stairs into the back parking lot. "That is the most handsome man I've ever seen, Evie, and he is totally in love with you! You lucky girl, you!"

I tried to speak but couldn't think of a thing to say. I was in shock.

By now, Hilly was getting in the driver's seat and I got in beside her with Slade riding shotgun. Mary and Bill were in the back seat, as usual.

"Okay, here we go then."

We were home in no time and everyone hiked up the path in silence. "This is it—Grey Boulders," Hilly announced.

We started climbing the stairs one by one and went around to the back door. "Drink, anyone?"

"Oh yes, please," everyone seemed to say at once.

"Help yourselves to the liquor cabinet, beer and mixers in the fridge. Slade, since you're our newest guest, I'll get yours."

"Beer is fine, thank you."

One-by-one, we found seats on the screened in porch that ran the length of the cottage. Huge green awnings hung over the many screens that kept the mosquitos away. It was quiet and lovely, plush furniture filled the room along with statues of Hilly's ancestors and two large, waist-high wicker plant pots holding giant ferns. It was an elegant space and this was only the second time we'd spent here.

Hilly sat near the glass slider presumably so she could play hostess more effectively.

I sat beside her on a wicker love seat with big, full

cushions. Slade sat beside me and Mary and Bill sat together on an oversized wicker chaise that was on the other side of the love seat.

"Can I get anything for anyone? Lobster salad? Crackers and cheese?"

"No, Hilly, relax. We're all fine and we're anxious to hear what happened to Slade."

"Pirates," he replied.

Everyone gasped.

"Tell us everything," Hilly said.

"Well, we were all asleep on the *Victoria E.,* a beautiful Bristol sailboat. I thought I heard something and looked out the porthole to see a boat rowing toward the bow of our boat. I grabbed Evie and unfortunately she hit her head on the doorway as I carried her to the stern and the dinghy. I woke Paddy and Bish but they were barely awake as the pirates came over the side of the boat. One guy was in the dinghy and we scuffled and he got cut with his knife. I got him out and I set the dinghy free. Paddy, Bish and I tried to radio for help and keep the pirates on the deck. But they got Bish so Paddy and I gave up. They took all our things and motored the boat to some mostly-deserted island up the coast.

"I'd stuffed Evie's things in my duffel and we all cooled our heels while arrangements were made with my father for our freedom. My father flew down, paid the ransom and the boat and all our stuff were returned unharmed. Paddy and Bish wanted to continue on after the cabin door was repaired and since the *Victoria E.* was actually my father's boat, he gave them his blessing.

"The reason no one knew anything about the incident was that my father handled everything privately. There was no press, no police, nothing that could affect the outcome of the kidnapping. He didn't want to take any chances. He is quite wealthy and used to doing things his way. Sometimes it is a bit trying and can be overwhelming, but I try to keep a low profile and stay out of the way.

"But when all was said and done, I did try to find Evie, of course. I didn't know what had happened to her and I feared the worst. Then, I heard from many native Bahamians about this girl from Maine trying to track down the *Victoria E.* and her crew.

"My father wanted me to return home with him, but for once I asserted myself as I was anxious to find Evie and make sure she was okay, as well as to return her things."

He winked at me.

"You have my things?" I could barely believe this was all true and Slade was here and okay.

"Yes, of course I do, Evie. You are very important to me and if I didn't know that when I was with you I sure did when I thought I'd lost you! I'm not taking any chances from now on. I'd like you at my side wherever I am for as long as I live."

I blushed and couldn't say anything. This was unbelievable!

"Well, I can take a hint," said Hilly. "I'm exhausted and I've got to get some sleep. You people and your adventures just wear me out," she laughed.

Bill and Mary were next to leave.

"Well, Evie, now tell me everything that's happened to you."

"Gee, Slade, if we're really going to have all this time together, shouldn't I save some of my stories for another day?" I smiled into his handsome face.

"Oh—yes. Well now that I know you are okay, I'd rather

kiss you anyway."

We talked and held each other and kissed. Suddenly I knew how Sir Walter felt about his wife and I knew that I could never be without Slade in my world. The only way I wouldn't want to live now was if I had to live without him.

Somewhere around 3 a.m. I embarked on a whole new avenue of my life, but as they say, *that's another story*. It was another part of my life that had been neglected and now I looked forward to making up for lost time. Slade was patient and tender and, "Oh Lord, he rocked my world!"

CHAPTER TWENTY-SEVEN

Slade and I had talked about what to do and where to go next but somehow all our plans and questions got lost in our first intimate moment. We never made it off the screened-in porch and awoke wrapped in each other's arms when the first shards of sunshine shot across the porch. Morning had arrived all too soon.

The sliding glass door from the dining room opened and Hilly's smiling face appeared.

"Breakfast is served. Come and get it—we have a big day planned!" Hilly laughed and was gone.

Slade and I looked at each other. I was thinking, "Were we staying? Were we going? Where? When?" And then I realized that I didn't need answers to those questions. I was with the best friends I'd ever had as well as the man I loved. I didn't have to worry now, just enjoy this summer paradise.

We had one of Hilly's fabulous salt-air brunches and made light conversation in between bites of toast, scrambled eggs, home fries, hot muffins, thick sliced ham and slab bacon and melon wedges. Overkill perhaps but that's what made Hilly's breakfasts legendary around these parts. This was just another reason why everyone adored her.

"There's some Korbel in the fridge if anyone's interested in a toast," Mary said when she saw me reach for the orange juice.

I laughed and said, "Why not?" and Mary immediately got the Champagne and popped the cork and set it in front of us on the table.

Slade started filling the glasses that Hilly and Bill put on the table and the drinks were passed around until everyone had one.

"To us and a new tradition!" Hilly said and drank deeply from her glass. "We'll have our new gang every summer for our annual outing. How's that sound?"

"Wonderful," I breathed and everyone turned and looked at me smiling.

"Well, there's more champers if you want to keep going or we could take Slade on a walking tour through the woods to the backshore." Hilly suggested.

That sounded perfect to all concerned so we set out as a group. The sun was never brighter and the sounds and smells were vibrant and sweet. Even the salt air was electric. I had never felt so alive, never felt so in love. Each moment with Slade was deeper and more intense than the last. I had no idea that I was capable of such feelings at this stage in my life. I was bursting with this new-found happiness.

We walked past the WW11 bunker and part way to the Ram Island Light House and stared at it as Hilly gave us chapter and verse on their history. Then we turned around and made our way back to the paths where the islanders cut from one part of the island to another without using the main roads. Slade and I trailed behind, holding hands and stealing kisses when no one was paying attention, which wasn't that often actually.

Every time Mary and Bill, very chummy themselves, looked at me and Slade they broke out laughing, causing us to laugh and Hilly to ask what was so funny.

It was a great morning constitutional and we all collapsed into the comfy deck chairs when we returned to Hilly's. What a spot. The gulls cawed and coasted overhead, lobster boats went about their business off Hilly's deck and the blue-diamond waters sparkled beyond the rocks. It was unadulterated perfection. For a moment I wondered about Micah and how his day was going.

Hilly was often saying, "There's nothing like Sterling's Island in the summer." Once more I looked around at the beautiful sights, and smelled the salt air and floral mix. She was so right.

We heard a lobster boat and an air horn and all went to the rail to see who was in front of the cottage. There was Micah sitting casually on the side of his boat with his feet on a rock poking out of the water. He looked so at ease as he balanced there keeping the boat from hitting the rocks in front of Hilly's. Obviously, he'd done this many, many times.

"Anyone for a ride?" He called up over the engine noise.

I looked at him with his muscular frame, blue eyes and sun-bleached red hair. If it weren't for my infatuation with Slade I wondered if I could have fallen in love with him, and thought, *guess we'll never know.*

"Me, I'll go, anyone else?" Hilly asked as she started down the steps.

We all looked at one another and smiled, content with our thoughts in our quiet, lazy deck chairs. No one made a move. And we soon heard Micah gun his engines and leave a wake as he headed down the bay with Hilly.

Sometime later we were getting hot under the noon sun. When someone suggested we return to the inner sanctum of the living room or the screened-in porch with its overstuffed cushions we all stood up and headed in immediately.

"Anyone hungry?" our consummate hostess poked her head around the corner and inquired and all we could do was groan in unison.

"Hey, when did you get back? Did you have fun?" Mary asked grinning like a Cheshire cat.

"Oh yes! Okay, later then," she responded and disappeared up the stairs to her bedroom.

"Hmmm," Bill pondered aloud, echoing all our thoughts.

Bill and Mary and Slade and I made our way to comfy chairs and were soon nodding off to nature's tunes—a slight breeze, ringing bell buoy and slapping waves.

It seemed like no time had passed before Hilly was back with her towel-wrapped head between the slider doors. "Hey, you guys, are you sleeping the day away?"

Everyone woke up and looked at her like she'd lost her mind or was pulling a bad practical joke. But Slade looked at his watch and exclaimed, "You're kidding, Hilly, we've been asleep for three hours?"

"Oh, yes. I've napped, showered and made reservations for us down the street. "Hurry up—we'll meet at the war wagon." She was gone.

"Oh, wow, there's cold beer in here," said Bill as he peered into the fridge. "Why don't you girls take your showers and Slade and I will visit a bit?"

With that, Mary and I raced up the carpeted stairs to the second floor. She headed for the bathroom while I wondered what on earth I'd wear. I didn't have that many clothes. Then I remembered the bag that Slade had brought for me from Nassau and I immediately busied myself looking through it for an outfit. I felt like I was preparing for my first date—again.

Days went by and we were having a ball. No one wanted it to end. Each day dawned beautiful. We took our group constitutional, returned for brunch or lunch and had cocktails on the deck before heading out to the various local watering holes. Some of the bars had entertainment. One of our favorite groups was playing at the 'Focile' so we tended to end up there to hear the music and it was the last stop before we all jumped or crawled to the war wagon and headed home for the night.

We saw a lot of Hilly's friends and noticed that Micah was usually turning up to join us for cocktails and the evening's activities. He and Slade got along particularly well so we weren't surprised when Slade announced one morning that he and Micah were off to explore the bay. When it happened a couple more times, we began to speculate on what could be so captivating there....

"Mermaids," Bill ventured.

"Oh sure, in this frigid water?" Hilly asked with a wide smile.

"Well, you just never know," Mary added. "Maybe Slade never had a lot of guy friends and he finally found one in Micah. I think it's neat."

"Me, too," we all agreed.

"Seriously, Hilly, where do you think they are going?"

"Oh, I don't know. Maybe they go down the bay and dig clams or something. Maybe Slade secretly wants to be a lobsterman and Micah's teaching him the ways of the waters for his new career."

For some reason we all howled at that response.

"Really, guys," Hilly said. "I don't know what's going on any more than you do."

But despite her denial, we all felt she knew exactly what was happening. *When would the rest of us be let in on the big secret,* we wondered to one another over the next few days. We had a lot of crazy ideas but no one could imagine a practical reason for these strange boating trips between Micah and Slade. They'd just take off and be gone for hours and then return with no explanation. And not once did they return with a bushel of freshly-dug clams.

We finally got tired of asking them why we couldn't go with them and what they were up to and we agreed to give up and adopt the 'wait and see' attitude.

CHAPTER TWENTY-EIGHT

"Another beautiful day! Let's get going!" Hilly exclaimed as we started to awaken bleary-eyed from our constant partying.

"Life is good." Slade whispered to me when Hilly pulled her head out of the room.

"I love you, Miss. Evie," Slade said softly and he kissed me deeply. I melted under his tender kiss—waiting and wanting his attention but not daring to respond or to initiate anything.

"Hey, get out of bed you two; today's a big day. We've got plans! Wear something casual!" Hilly said as she poked her head back into the room.

"What?" I squealed as Slade was suddenly up and pulling me out of bed and into his arms. He kissed me quickly and was off to the shower leaving me to rummage through my bag and find something "casual". The problem wasn't so much finding something casual but finding something that was also clean.

I'd been washing my things out in the sink and hanging

them to dry during my stay with Hilly but since Slade had arrived, I found that I didn't have the time or forethought to rinse out my clothes every night.

"Wow!" I pulled out the sleeveless white blouse and my old yellow culottes that I'd worn a lot in Nassau. They made me smile when I saw them. I'd come a long way since the days on Paradise Island and sailing with Slade and Bish and Paddy in the beautiful *Victoria E.* I dearly missed that time and the wonderful company.

I fished around for the broach and was heartened when I felt its familiar shape. I thought of pinning it to my collar but changed my mind and put it back safely in its special spot in my bag. I patted it gently and withdrew my hand and closed the bag.

"Next," Slade said as he poked his head in the door. "I've got to make a call so I'm going downstairs. This is going to be a great day, Evie," he said and was gone when I turned to respond.

I hung my clothes over the towel rack while I showered. Luckily, the trick had worked and when I got through with the long, hot shower, my clothes were relatively wrinkle-free. I shook them just to take out any lingering wrinkles.

When I got downstairs, everyone was gathered in the kitchen as usual. But today there was no cooking and no hot dishes on the table and none of the usual hustle and bustle that accompanied one of Hilly's famous brunches. There was a large basket on the sideboard and what seemed like a lot of excited people ready for an adventure.

Just then we heard the air horn and Hilly said, "Let's go!" and we proceeded to go out the side door, onto the deck, down the long stairs and then the rock stairs to Micah and his waiting boat. There he was as usual, sitting on the gunnels and fending the boat off the rocks with his feet. Looking comfortable and natural as could be....

Micah greeted each of us and helped us aboard one-by-one and when we were all safely aboard the boat, he gave the boat a push from the rock, grabbed the controls and we were off in an instant.

Three minutes later, we were pulling into the back cove of what I'd been told was a deserted island.

"Where are we? What's this?" Bill asked first.

I turned to Slade who was beside me.

"This is Tabor Island and we were told it was a wedding present," Micah and Hilly offered.

There was a sudden hush and all we could hear were the waves gently slapping against the side of the boat.

"What?" Mary, Bill and I asked in unison.

"Will you marry me, Miss Evie?" Slade asked. He was on his knees before me.

I could feel myself getting weak in the knees and the heat rising on my neck. My face was flushed in spite of the nice wind that was keeping us cool on this hot summer day. My mind was racing; my head was spinning.

"Are you going to say *yes?*" Slade asked anxiously.

"I, I, I...," I stammered. I was so shocked I couldn't talk. This was the last thing I expected.

Then I noticed that Slade was holding an open ring box in his right hand. I looked at the magnificent diamond ring sparkling in the sunlight—pure perfection. For some insane reason all I could think about was that I was glad I hadn't pinned the family broach to my collar!

"Well?" he asked. " I love you very much, you know. Will you be my wife, Evie, and stay with me forever?"

"Oh, my Lord... I, well," I managed to say.

"Just say it!" someone said.

"Yeah, answer the man for heaven's sake, Evie. We can't stand this!"

"Yes," I said with my last breath. I don't think I was breathing from the time he proposed....

There was a huge cheer and Slade was lifting me off the deck and twirling me around. He kissed me tenderly and smiled into my glistening eyes. I didn't even realize I was crying tears of joy.

"Thank you, Evie. You won't be sorry. I love you so," he whispered in my ear as he carefully brushed the tears from my cheeks.

I had goose-bumps all over me.

Everyone crowded around us, laughing, hugging. We were all giddy with excitement. Just then we caught a wake broadside and everyone was suddenly quiet as they tried to keep their balance. Slade drew me to him to steady me.

Just then I noticed two familiar figures and I almost fainted. There, holding onto the side rail were Paddy and Bish, looking fantastic. They were all smiles.

"Congratulations in order, then?" they asked.

"Oh yes!" I managed to say and then realized everyone was grabbing at my hand to look at my engagement ring. I hadn't even realized Slade had slipped it on—such was my state.

"Well, let's go look at the island. Climb aboard," Bish said.

We climbed over the rail and into the runabout that was alongside.

Soon, we were on the island, drinking Mimosas from the large basket and eating finger sandwiches and pickles and chips. There was a large table set up in the cove with quite a spread already set out.

We all laughed when we spotted a freshly cooked bushel of steamers at the beginning of the table. It had become quite a joke over the last few days.

People came out of nowhere to serve food and drink. *Where did they come from and how did they get here?* I wondered.

"The *Victoria E.* is on the other side of the island. We used her to shuttle everyone back and forth while we set up for this affair. We are roasting a pig in the BBQ pit and later we'll have lobsters and more champagne!" Hilly told us excitedly.

"Wow," was all Bill and Mary could manage. "This is really something!"

Slade and I were talking with Bill and Mary, Hilly and Micah and Paddy and Bish. We were introducing everyone and just trying to hug our long-lost friends and catch up on the past weeks. We were having the most wonderful time imaginable.

I didn't notice Paddy and Bish slip away, but all of a sudden I heard all this commotion and hollering. Everyone turned to see the funniest sight: There in front of us, coming from the *Victoria E.*, was this great golden lab galloping toward us at top speed. She was straining her green collar and leash to the breaking point and Bish was holding on for all she was worth. Bish was so tiny and her feet were flying so fast I thought she might fall or be launched into the air any second. She was yelling, "Emma, Emma, whoa! Stop! Slow down...arrrggghhh...." Behind her, Paddy was trying his best to call the dog and catch up with the rest of his family.

What a sight! That dog would have done an Ididarod Husky proud. She was flying down the wharf with the ocean and majestic boat in the background, and I was lost for a second by this unfolding scene. Slade, though, had his wits about him and jumped up and intercepted the dog.

"I guess the leash was a mistake," gasped Bish as Slade bent down to pet the dog, collar in hand.

"This is our dog, Emma," Bish managed, still catching her breath.

We gathered 'round, laughing and petting the beautiful dog, who wasn't even panting after that bounding romp.

"She's been pent up on the boat for awhile, I guess?" asked Slade.

"No, you'd think so, but she's always like this. We took her out this morning and she ran all over the island before we started setting up and ferrying people over. When she laid down exhausted after charging around for an hour we thought she'd catch up on her rest."

"Apparently she has," I added, still laughing. We all roared at that as Paddy and Bish walked Emma back to the boat.

As the afternoon progressed, Slade and I noticed that Micah and Hilly had disappeared and Bill and Mary were sitting in quiet conversation on one of the outcroppings of rocks. It was plain to see they were now madly in love. I admitted to Slade that I never saw that coming as we watched them touching and talking like they were the only people on earth.

"Where do you suppose Hilly and Micah are?" I asked Slade.

He smiled and said, "Well, I don't know anything except love seems to be in the air."

"What? Do you think we started something here?" I almost screamed.

Slade burst out laughing.

"Another one you didn't see coming, huh?" he smiled good naturedly.

"Oh my Lord, you could say that. Well, he's quite a guy. I might have been interested in him if I hadn't been pining away for you, you know."

"You're kidding right?" he asked.

While I was trying to figure out how to respond, he saved me.

"You were pining for me? Really?"

We both broke out in uncontrolled laughter.

When I finally got hold of myself and could control my voice, I added, "Good. I am very happy for them—they make a great pair!"

Slade laughed. "You gals aren't the only ones who can scheme and put a plan together, you know."

"This is crazy, wonderful, unbelievable, my word I am totally at a loss here." I looked at him and then glanced around at the growing crowd.

"Yeah, we thought we'd have an 'intention celebration' today and make the announcement over lobster, roast pig and champagne."

He could see that I was speechless so he continued, "We thought we'd get together and decide who wanted a big event or if everyone wants a quiet 'do' then we'll make the arrangements and then throw one hell of a wedding reception at some convenient time down the road.

"My parents gave us the *Victoria E.*, a townhouse and some other assets as wedding presents. I thought we could all build houses here on the shore and then have a central communal place in the middle of the island. We can use the huge WWII installation as a foundation and build a 'great house' on top of it. You know like the one they did on

Sterling's Island. We can store all our provisions and supplies in the cool rooms and tunnels and on top we'll build a major kitchen. We will have a terrific fireplace and lots of tables, overstuffed chairs and couches, card tables, a large dining table—you know, something that could accommodate a UN delegation. Just kidding about that, but not about the extra-long table—seating for forty, at least. We can work out the details later. What do you think?"

"I'm stunned; I don't think I can think at this point," I answered. "But it does sound so fabulous. We'd be with all our best friends. We could stay here at least during the summers and all be together. If the world blows up and the way things are going I'm not ruling that out—we can all gather here for support and companionship."

"We'll run cables from Cat Island and get fresh water and phones and other communications. We'll use the wells here after we have them checked out—they haven't been used for years. We'll get satellite dishes for all the televisions and we'll have cell phones and all the latest technology to keep track of global events."

"Can we have a salt water swimming pool? And Hilly will want a tennis court," I was beginning to find my voice and I was excited.

"My dear, I don't believe that you haven't guessed it by now but we can have anything we want." He smiled at me lovingly.

I couldn't believe it. I was still looking at my ring every chance I got in different positions and sunlight and shade. I even put my hand in a shallow tidal pool to see how it shimmered and sparkled in the ocean water—pure perfection—like Slade. It took my breath away.

"Do you want to join everyone now and see where we

go from here?" he asked.

"Do I? You bet I do!" I stared at him and again he leaned over and kissed me.

"I do love you, Slade," I said and I knew he would make me happy for the rest of my life. I just didn't know what I'd done to deserve this man. I didn't know but I wasn't going to worry about it. I'd just make him as happy as I could and thank my lucky stars that the dangling wire didn't have enough juice to kill me.

"Let's go," I said as I grabbed his hand. "I can't wait to find the others!"

Slade pointed to an osprey nest atop an old light pole and we craned our necks to see the bird sitting on her eggs. Birds glided over head on currents of ocean air. The sun shine was warm and therapeutic and the island flowers were breathtakingly beautiful and scented.

This was the best day I'd ever had. Life was perfect. I couldn't have imagined a better ending!

THE END

Other Books by PR Hersey

Romance and Action, Mystery

Company Men -2006

The Devil's Insider -2004

The Takedown* -2000, Reprint 2006

More Company Men: Global Dawn

Children's Books
(available from author only, at this time)

Ralphy, Tom and Billy
The Trouble with Terrence
Horace the Hermit Crab
Zeb and Fred
On an Island

---

*   *"...the romance/murder mystery...is all about fun and games. Smoke carries a trusty forty-four. His gorgeous dead wife Catherine has cast a shadow across his future that only the love of a good woman can heal. There is the conniving boss, Barry Crumblick and a detective named Peter Murchee, aka "Murch". What's not to like?"*

—Maine Sunday Telegram

The Takedown Series

After the *Takedown Trilogy*—*The Takedown, Devil's Insider,* and *Company Men*—comes more murder mystery action with Smoke, Vicky and the gang. Most action will take place around Washington, D.C. and my beloved home state of Maine with a particular emphasis on the Casco Bay Islands.

This book, too, is a work of fact and fiction—*More Company Men: Global Dawn.* It involves some of today's hot topics: Medicare, government healthcare, insurance companies, the medical profession, government corruption, special interest groups—the whole gamut—in a fast-paced murder mystery by PRHersey. I hope you'll join me for the ride!

Author's Note:

The Dangling Wire is a romantic adventure, a complete departure from my previous works. But everyone who likes adventure and would like to revisit their first love or who just likes love stories with adventure and 'local color' will, I believe, find this a good and fun read.

PR Hersey

PR Hersey, a lifelong resident of Portland and Peaks Island, Maine, spent thirteen years as an M.T. (A.S.C.P.) Microbiologist and Laboratory Supervisor in the medical arena. She then changed her career path and entered the world of insurance.

During the eighties and nineties, she worked for the top two LTD (long term disability) reinsurance companies in the country. She worked in every area of the field, i.e., underwriting, marketing, competitive intelligence, contracts, filing and compliance, legal documents, product development and exploration of foreign markets. She also edited a reinsurance newsletter and wrote for professional publications such as *The New England Journal of Insurance Medicine.*

Since retiring from the insurance business in 2003, she has been concentrating on writing and consulting for people who need her expertise, especially in the area of disability. A practicing Notary Public and Dedimus Justice, she keeps busy with her family and rescued lab, Emma.